The
Blind
Melody

GARY LEE VINCENT

Burning Bulb
PUBLISHING

The Blind Melody
By **Gary Lee Vincent**

Burning Bulb Publishing
P.O. Box 4721
Bridgeport, WV 26330-4721
United States of America
www.BurningBulbPublishing.com

Cover designed by Melissa St. Giles.

First Edition.

Paperback Edition ISBN: 978-1-948278-74-4

Also by Gary Lee Vincent

Novels
PASSAGEWAY
BELLY TIMBER
ATTACK OF THE MELONHEADS
WHEN THE BEDPOSTS SHAKE (RING OF THE SUCCUBUS)
IMPOUND
STRANGE FRIENDS

Darkened—The West Virginia Vampire Series
DARKENED HILLS
DARKENED HOLLOWS
DARKENED WATERS
DARKENED SOULS
DARKENED MINDS
DARKENED DESTINIES

The Douglas River Vampire Series
RIVER: A VAMPIRE'S NIGHTMARE
ICARUS

The Black Circle Chronicles
PROVE YOUR LOVE
STRANGE NEW POWERS
NIGHT WINGS
SHEEP AMONGST WOLVES
LORD OF THE BIRDS

Crackimals
CRACKCOON
CRACKODILE
CRACKSQUATCH

Dedicated to
Melissa Hallmark

PART ONE:
ADRIANA

OVERTURE

The gunshot rang out, having prominence over everything else in the world at that moment.

Adriana froze; time froze. Then, time froze again because another gunshot followed the first. Both from the same gun.

The first gunshot was fatal; the second almost as fatal, having consequences that lasted from that evil moment to the present time.

CHAPTER 1

Adriana Fernandez worked at Casa de Carlito, a jazz venue in downtown Belém. This port city was the gateway to the Amazon River and the capital of the Brazilian state of Pará.

Adriana had been born in Belém and lived there all her twenty-eight years. There was little to tell about her family that couldn't be said about thousands of other poor Brazilian families, and everything could be summed up in that one word: 'poverty.' She'd been just another young Brazilian woman, attractive, educated, and determined but bogged down by a system that seemed designed to prevent her from accomplishing anything of value.

Adriana had loved music from a very early age, dancing and singing to her parents' CD collection and the radio. In elementary school, dancing and singing were as far as it went. But when she got to high school, her parents paid for some piano lessons for her, and from that moment on, she never looked back.

By the time she was twenty, she was an excellent jazz and samba pianist. She also had a good singing voice and had played in several local bands. Lots of her friends told her she was good enough to make it big, and she'd tried to get herself into the limelight, but success continued to elude her.

"It isn't that you're not good enough," her father often told her. "It's just that Brazil is full of talented young musicians and singers, and this new reliance on the internet for everything has just made things worse." Then he'd smile—his prematurely-aged face momentarily brightening—and add, "But keep striving, girl. Someday, your own benevolent star will shine down on you."

Adriana's father had been a laborer at the Belém docks. He'd worked his fingers to the bone to put food on their table and then, three years ago, had suddenly dropped dead from a heart attack while single-handedly carrying a crate meant to be moved by three men.

In a burdened and struggling economy where jobs were almost as scarce as unicorns, deaths from overwork were a common enough occurrence. Carlos Fernandez's death was nothing special. A pittance was paid as compensation to his family. The dead man was stuck in the ground. A priest said a few prayers over his grave, and that was it.

Adriana and her kid brother Mario were left without a father, their mother Bruna was left without her husband, and the family was left to soldier on as best they could, which wasn't very well. But still, they made do.

Bruna Fernandez had always been a sickly woman. She'd been born poor and, in addition to remaining poor, had never managed to pull herself out of the miry mindset of never having enough. Like many of her poor neighbors, a tapestry of suffering was etched in her face. She did some cleaning work for the wealthier citizens, but Bruna was too frail to exert herself for long periods, and even when she could work, these jobs really didn't pay all that much.

Noticing how sickly she seemed to be getting, her two children began nagging her to reduce her workload lest she exit life as summarily as her husband had. Bruna protested, but in the end, she had no natural choice. Ultimately, she consented to her children's requests and stayed home, making straw hats for sale to laborers.

It thus fell on Adriana and Mario to keep the household going. It helped that, at the moment, Adriana had just begun playing in a band at Casa de Carlito.

The club was small, and the pay wasn't much to write home about, but she had her days free to pursue her music and any other activities she desired.

In vain, she tried looking for work, something she could do alongside her music. She did a stint or two as a waitress, but the rotating shifts kept conflicting with either band practices or band performances, and in the end, she had to give it up.

Adriana felt good about this new band, which they had named Sistema de Música. They were tight and had a solid repertoire, and she felt that if they could hold it together for a while, they had an excellent chance of making it to the big leagues.

In addition to this, Adriana was sweet on Gabriel, the band's leader and trumpet player. She and Gabriel weren't dating yet, but it was just a matter of time.

At that same point, when Adriana's father died, her brother Mario had been preparing to enter university. Seeing as getting any kind of scholarship was out of the question, Mario had been doing any sort of odd job he could to save money for tuition fees, books, and living expenses. Adriana, too, had been putting aside the little she could to help him achieve his goal of studying medicine. Mario had just turned eighteen at the time, so when one of the waiters at Casa de Carlito quit over a pay dispute, Adriana had suggested him for the job. The pay wasn't a lot, but it added to what he was earning from his myriad day jobs. Mario was also popular with the gangsters who frequented the club, and sometimes they gave him generous tips.

So, things trudged on slowly, with the Fernandez family feeling cautiously optimistic about their future.

***

That Saturday night began like any other night. Casa de Carlito was packed for a change. Lots of drinking and rowdiness, lots of dancing and romancing was going on. A good number of tonight's patrons were gangsters, but they weren't here to make trouble; rival factions sat in opposite corners of the club, occasionally acknowledging each other with tough-guy sneers and mocking laughter. Once in a while, a member of one of the gangs yelled out a drunken insult at their rivals, but what they'd said was swallowed up in the noise of the room and the sound of the band. Most of the time, the gangster factions couldn't even visually make out their rivals; there were too many people in the way.

Mario and the other two waiters were kept busy running up and down the room, ferrying drinks and the occasional sandwich from the bar to the tables.

Adriana was up on stage doing a solo number with the drummer and bass player. This happened occasionally if the brass players felt they needed a break or when the main singer, Marcella, had just gotten through a set of particularly demanding songs. At such times, Adriana got the spotlight for a few minutes. Most times, she just sang pop ballads, and that's what she did tonight:

"I'm dreaming of a bright, lo-oove-ly future,
An uncertain future, still out of view,
But a pure and happy one for me and for you,
Where we will love one another all the day through..."

She'd written the song one morning when she had been thinking about her crush, Gabriel, the trumpet player, and Mario had teasingly helped her with the lyrics.

And then the trouble started.

As was to be expected, the trouble started from the gangs. Jane, the girlfriend of a burly gangster named Renato Barbosa, a member of the gang called *Os Vermelhos* or 'The Red Ones,' had previously left his side to visit the ladies' room. Now, as she and another woman were returning to their table, their way was blocked by Joao Ramires, a gangster from a different faction called *As Cobras Negras*—The Black Snakes. Joao Ramires was tall and ugly and had a well-deserved reputation for meanness.

Unfortunately for Jane and her girlfriend, the route back to their company passed about a yard from the intoxicated Joao, and so, suddenly, there he was standing in front of them.

"I like this song the songbird is singing," he told Jane, showering her with a rain of alcoholic fumes and some spit. "You must dance with me tonight."

Although he totally disgusted Jane, she was also very scared of him, and so she tried not to offend him. "I'm sorry, Joao, but I'm here with Renato." She smiled. "You know how jealous he gets if he sees me dancing with another man, particularly one as good-looking as yourself."

After stating this, Jane looked at her friend Maria for confirmation. Maria nodded her head vigorously. "It is so, Joao. You know it is so."

Joao considered himself more sophisticated than most. He had traveled a lot and had a brother, Ricardo, who lived in the United States of America. In addition, he spoke a little English. Most of the club patrons only spoke Portuguese. Adriana's own proper knowledge of English mostly came from the two years she'd spent as a music teacher at an international school. The rest (including most of the slang she knew) had been gleaned from mingling with itinerant American and British musicians. She'd taken learning English seriously, believing it would help her musical career.

Now, Joao Ramires was also a ladies' man, a man used to having his way with women. But even so, had he not been so drunk, he would never have attempted to dance with Jane that night, definitely not with her boyfriend and her boyfriend's gang mates in the same bar.

But tonight, the alcohol was red in Joao's eyes, and he did not care.

"Renato will have to wait his turn," he told Jane with a broad leer and a tipsy bow. "This slow music of Adriana's reminds me of love. I must dance to it with you."

Jane's friend Maria tried to intervene, but Joao ended her protest with a shove that sent her into Mario and caused him to spill his tray of drinks.

Mario turned around angrily and then saw what was happening, which was how he became involved in the whole affair. Adriana, however, hadn't noticed a thing. She was away in an alternate musical world, eyes closed in rapture, her fingers pounding the keys of her electric piano, and her voice expressing her desire that someday soon:

"Despite our shaky start,
You and I,
That special guy I desire with my whole heart,
Will live together in a place where we will never part."

Meanwhile, trouble was brewing. One of Renato's friends had pointed out Jane and Joao on the dance floor. Renato Barbosa, who was almost as drunk as Joao, had stumbled to his feet and walked over to retrieve his woman, shoving both patrons and waiters out of the way. Renato's reputation was almost as bad as Joao's, with the result that by the time he arrived where Jane was fiercely trying to pry herself away from Joao, and avoid his questing lips, the dancefloor was almost empty of people.

Adriana was just finishing her song. She opened her eyes and saw the two men approaching a collision. She leaned back from the microphone and gaped.

"Let my woman go, you dog!" Renato Barbosa told Joao, flashing a switchblade at him.

"Am I supposed to be scared by that?" Joao laughed in his face, and then he pushed Jane aside, where she stood, wiping his spit off of her cheeks and hoping that Renato would give him a good beating.

Mario had now reached the two men. "Calm down, calm down," he exhorted them while their respective gangs watched, expecting some entertaining but relatively harmless bloodshed. There was a hush in the bar, with everyone waiting expectantly to see what would happen. The bartender had already departed into the back to fetch the proprietor to come help defuse the tense situation.

On any other night, maybe nothing would have happened. But tonight, maybe both men were too drunk, or maybe Jane's large bosom was a larger bone of contention between them than the watchers realized. Or maybe this was simply the night when the usual territorial rivalries over drugs and prostitution were destined to come to a head.

Whatever the case, Joao spat in Renato's face. "Go to hell, dog!"

There was an instant hush in the bar, and then Renato lunged at Joao with the switchblade aimed at his face.

Mario intervened in time and stopped Renato from stabbing Joao. But what Mario didn't realize was that Joao was armed, too. Joao was carrying a gun, which he pulled out now.

Joao fired twice. "Die, bastard! And after your funeral, your sweet Jane will be mine for good!"

The first bullet hit Mario, the second hit Renato Barbosa, or maybe the order was the other way around. Both shot men fell to the ground, and everyone who hadn't been shot began shouting something or other, with Adriana screaming the loudest as she leaped down from the stage and ran onto the dance floor.

CHAPTER 2

Once safely outside Casa de Carlito, Joao Ramires cursed silently in the night.

Joao was still too drunk to appreciate the full implications of his murderous actions, but even so, he knew he'd just made a bad mistake.

The wailing coming from inside the nightclub—with Jane's voice screaming loudest of all—let him know that tonight he'd really messed up.

Before his gang buddies David and Pedro had rushed him through the startled and confused audience to his murderous actions and hustled him out of the club, Joao had gotten a good look at Renato: the son-of-a-bitch was dead like the dirty pig he was. Joao didn't at all regret shooting Renato—it was long overdue to show him who was boss in this section of Belém. Joao had no idea what a pretty woman like Jane had ever seen in Renato.

But shooting the waiter Mario had been a mistake, a complication they didn't need.

Well, at least the kid didn't appear to be dead, too.

Joao considered all of this in a drunken rush as the noise from the club pursued him and his companions while they hurried down the dark aisles between several of the buildings flanking Casa de Carlito and the noise of the rear highway grew closer, with both the former and the latter punctuated by the sounds of television and of family quarrels and of drunken buddies playing checkers and arguing over nothing important.

Meanwhile, Joao's gang members, David and Pedro, were nervous as they fled the scene of the crime. "Come on, come on, move it, Joao!

11

We need to get you away from here before the police arrive!" David urged.

Joao nodded as their urgency communicated itself to him. Their quartet moved off, keeping in the shadows between the buildings and ducking low where light spilled from too many windows. Joao made out the distant sound of sirens.

The police had arrived.

Pedro rushed forward to the end of the aisle they were currently passing through. After peeking cautiously left and right, he nodded back at them.

"Coast is clear. Hurry up, and let's get the hell away from here."

CHAPTER 3

Adriana was in shock, unable to believe what had just transpired right before her eyes. She knelt on the dancefloor, holding Mario's shoulders. Around her and her wounded brother, the club was in almost total pandemonium and loud confusion that had resulted from the shooting incident.

Everyone, Adriana included, seemed unsure what to do. A shooting like this had never happened before in Casa de Carlito.

"Mario, Mario, are you okay!?" Adriana asked him. The question seemed to her a silly one, as she could see the blood streaming from his body. But at least he was in better condition than Renato Barbosa, who lay stone-dead beside him. Several tipsy members of *Os Vermelhos* were still trying to rouse Renato, but it was an exercise in futility. Renato's eyes were wide open, and he kept staring, staring at nothing, his once vigorous form motionless.

Jane, the cause of the argument between Renato and his killer, had fainted; two of her girlfriends were trying to rouse her. There were also cellphone camera flashes as people took pictures of the gory scene.

"Where is that bastard Joao?" angry voices asked around Adriana.

"He's fled, he's fled!" a woman replied. "Oh, he killed two people and ran away."

"Shut up, puta!" a man growled at the female speaker. "You weren't here! You didn't see what happened!"

"How do you feel?" Adriana asked Mario. He nodded but couldn't talk. She held his hand tight. "Just hold on, little brother, hold on. You'll be okay."

The confusion still raged around them, with half-drunken revelers shouting to make themselves heard over the other club patrons. No one seemed to have thought to call for an ambulance, but several of the shadier patrons had already realized the police would soon be arriving at Casa de Carlito and were fast departing the scene.

Then Adriana felt a hand on her shoulder. She looked up and saw that it was Gabriel, the band's leader and trumpeter. Their drummer, Lucas, and bass player, Daniel, were both with him.

"We need to get Mario to a hospital," she told Gabriel in a trembling voice and with intense worry in her eyes.

Gabriel nodded; he looked as just as worried as Adriana did, and she knew why that was. Mario looked like he was dying. His face was a pale shadow of its usual color and liveliness. And there was also the widening pool of blood around him that was seemingly leaking from his back.

Gabriel gestured quickly over to the bar, where Adriana saw that the club owner, Carlito, was staring in disgust at his cell phone while shaking it. "He's been trying to get an ambulance, but the lines are jammed."

"We'll have to take the band's van," Daniel, the bass player, said.

"Help me lift him up," Adriana said.

She wanted to help the men, but they shook their heads. "Get your handbag and meet us outside," Gabriel told her.

Adriana nodded, and after sparing a moment to watch the three men lift Mario up and make their way with him through the crowd of witnesses, she hurried over to the bandstand and grabbed her purse. Then she dashed after the others.

By the time she reached Gabriel's white van, the men had laid Mario on the floor in its empty rear section.

Adriana quickly climbed into the van beside Mario, and they set off.

***

Even though the Mercy Hospital was only a short distance away from Casa de Carlito, that drive along the night-shrouded streets of downtown Belém was the longest of Adriana's life. Seated there on the floor in the rear of the van, with Mario's hand clasped in hers, and all the while praying that he'd survive. Every few seconds, she shook Mario gently to ensure that he remained awake.

She had no idea what she would do if he died. *Oh, my God, what in the world will I tell Mama if that happens? For her, just hearing that he's been shot will be bad enough, but to hear that he's dead?*

"Are we there yet?" she shouted forward at the others, who were sharing the front of the van. The rear of the van had no windows, and she had no idea how far they'd proceeded on their frantic journey.

"Almost!" Gabriel called back at her, his voice as urgent as hers. "How is he?"

"I don't know, Gabriel! He looks like he's dying!" Adriana called back in a wavering voice. "Just go as fast as you can! Please!"

Her desperate, impassioned plea was followed by a burst of speed from the van, and a few seconds later, she was almost thrown over as the vehicle swerved violently and then came abruptly to a halt.

"We've arrived," Gabriel announced.

Then came the rush of the men leaping out of the van. When Daniel opened the rear doors for Adriana, she saw Gabriel and Lucas dashing through the doors of the ER, which was maybe twenty yards away from their parking space. Then, a few moments later, they remerged in the company of a group of medics who were rolling a stretcher towards her.

The group quickly arrived at the van, and the medics lifted Mario out of the rear and laid him on the stretcher.

"He's still alive," one of the medics told Adriana as they wheeled Mario away. Adriana went with them, holding Mario's hand, though his grip was extremely weak if he had any grip at all.

"His pulse is still strong," the doctor who quickly examined Mario said. "He should be okay. But he needs surgery right away."

Adriana, Gabriel, and the two other band members waited on a long-padded bench in an antiseptic-smelling and brightly lit corridor while Mario was wheeled away for emergency surgery.

"I need to call my mother," Adriana told the guys, pulling out her cell phone while saying so.

"Don't," Gabriel advised. "Not till we know Mario's condition. Wait till the surgery is over."

"Why not?"

"Your old mother might drop dead of a heart attack if you give her such bad news over the phone," Daniel piped in. "Or she'll come over here and start wailing her lungs out."

"Yeah," Gabriel agreed. "What if she dies of a heart attack and Mario is later okay?"

Adriana really wanted to make that phone call to her mother, but she decided her friends were right. She put the phone away and hugged herself like she was feeling cold, though the hospital corridor was quite warm.

"I still can't believe what happened at the club tonight," she said.

"How on earth could Joao snap like that?" Gabriel asked. "Yes, everyone knows that he's a hothead, but to go so far as shooting Renato dead?" Gabriel gestured down the corridor in the direction that the doctors had wheeled Mario. "And then he shot Mario, too."

"The police will soon be here," Lucas said. "What are we going to tell them?"

"Nothing," Gabriel said. "We were all busy playing our music, and we didn't see what happened."

"I know I didn't," Lucas said. "There were too many people standing in the way. Even after I heard the gunshots, I thought one of the loudspeakers was malfunctioning."

"Me too," Daniel agreed. "I thought my bass amp had overloaded again and blown up."

"I saw everything that took place," Adriana said in a cold voice that nevertheless dripped with fury. "I'm not going to let Joao get away with this. He can't get away with this."

Gabriel shook his head. "No, Addy, leave Joao alone. You know as well as I do that that is the wise thing to do. Otherwise, the gangsters will come after you. So long as the doctors save Mario's life, it is best to let sleeping dogs lie. Let *Os Vermelhos* handle their revenge their own way."

"I can't." Adriana resisted the wisdom of Gabriel's words. She was still too worried and angered by what had happened to think straight. In her angered state it sounded cowardly to keep mute after witnessing a murder being committed.

Gabriel's cellphone buzzed then. He took it out of his pocket and studied its screen, then looked at his companions. "It's a text from Joey. He says the police are asking which hospital we took Mario too." Joey was Sistema de Música's guitarist.

Adriana shook her head. "You know, I really don't feel up to talking to them tonight. Not with my younger brother still in a critical condition."

"Me neither," Daniel said, with Lucas also nodding his agreement.

Gabriel shrugged. "You're reading my mind as well. Hold on, while I reply Joey." After thinking for a moment, he tapped off a reply on his cellphone, then leaned back with a look of satisfaction on his face. "That's done then."

"Did you give them the name of this place?" Adriana asked worriedly.

Gabriel shook his head and cracked a weak smile. "No, I didn't, Addy. I told Joey to tell them we went to that big Saint Jude's Hospital near the petrol station where his dad works."

"But that's halfway across town!" Lucas pointed out, getting up from his place on their bench and moving to lean against the opposite wall of the corridor.

"Exactly," Gabriel agreed. "If the police think we're over *there*, they won't come *here* looking for us."

"At least not until the hospital files their official report about Mario's gunshot wound," Adriana agreed. "Which won't happen till morning." She smiled gratefully at Gabriel. "Thanks, man."

"Don't mention it. Having the police here now will just be a hassle."

The four young Brazilian musicians broke off their conversation as the double doors at the right end of the corridor swung open.

A middle-aged nurse emerged from the doors, pushing a medical cart before her. They looked at her expectantly, hoping she had some news of Mario's condition for them, but she seemed not to know what they were there for, and walked past them with only the vaguest of greeting nods in their direction.

Disappointed and at the same time relieved, they put their minds back to the knotty issue of what to tell the police.

"Yeah, Addy, you know that keeping mute about this is the right thing to do," Gabriel said after a while. "Just keep silent about this like everyone else will certainly do."

Adriana shook her head. She had no doubt that Gabriel was right, that 'keeping silent' was what just about everyone at the club tonight would do. And, in reality, this stance had nothing to do with cowardice. It was simply the rule of the streets. The gangsters would sort themselves out, most likely in a short-term gang war. The one exception who could be expected to tell the police exactly what had happened tonight would be Renato Barbosa's girlfriend Jane, who was known to be passionately in love with him. Maybe Carlito might say something too; but Adriana doubted this.

Yes, Gabriel is right, she thought to herself. *So long as Mario suffers no permanent hurt, I too will pretend that I never saw what happened tonight.*

Externally, however, she merely nodded at Gabriel.

Several doctors and nurses passed them by without comment during the next hour while Adriana sat nervously with her hands clasped in her lap. The more time that passed without anyone bringing news of Mario to her, the more anxious she grew, though she concealed her worry as best she could. Occasionally, Gabriel squeezed her arm to reassure her.

"Mario will be fine," he and the others all told her, but she could see that they too were very worried about her brother.

"Why is there so much delay then?" she asked in an anguished voice, her eyes darting towards the double doors that led towards the surgery. She then got to her feet and began pacing agitatedly back and forth along the corridor, till finally she tired of doing this and sat down again. She felt a deep need to burst into tears again but managed to hold the tears back.

It was maybe fifteen minutes after this outburst of hers, that the surgeon who'd accompanied Mario to the operating theater finally made his appearance again. He had sweat on his brow and a frown on his face that made Adriana's heart lurch.

Once the surgeon had emerged through the double doors, he headed directly for the small group of worried musicians. They in turn left their standing and sitting positions and walked over to meet him.

"The surgery went well," the doctor told them, with a tight-lipped smile. He looked searching at Adriana. "You can relax for now; your younger brother is out of danger."

Adriana heaved a deep sigh of relief. However, she still sensed something very bothersome in the doctor's frown; something more than mere exhaustion, and she wondered what that could possibly be.

"There were however a few complications," the surgeon began saying. But then, before he could explain in detail, a portly elderly nurse whom Adriana recognized as the hospital matron suddenly appeared at the other end of the corridor.

"Dr. Sanchez, Dr. Sanchez," she called out in an agitated voice, while waving furiously towards him. "Please come quick, we've a stab wound victim."

The doctor nodded back at her, and then told Adriana and her friends. "Sorry, but I can't say more about the complication now." His gaze once more focused on Adriana. "Please come here tomorrow morning with your parents and I'll explain in detail."

"He isn't brain-dead, is he?" she in turn asked, though she saw no way how that could be the case, as Joao hadn't shot her brother in the head.

The doctor managed a smile. "No, nothing as serious as that. Just come in the morning like I said."

"Can we see Mario now?" Gabriel asked.

The matron was still waiting at the end of the corridor. The doctor had already begun walking away, but he paused to reply to Gabriel's question. "Best you leave it till morning. He's still unconscious because of the anesthetic."

With that he was gone, and the four young musicians could now relax a little.

"Thank God that Mario pulled through," Lucas said.

"Yes, thank God," Adriana said. "But what on earth does he mean by complications? I hope the bullet didn't destroy one of Mario's kidneys. That would be just horrible."

In reply to that, her friends could only stare at her worriedly.

"Well, we all heard the doctor," Gabriel said after a while. "They won't let us see Mario tonight, so I'll drive us back to the club so we can pack up our gear and call it a night."

They left the hospital, with Adriana both leaving her phone number with the nurses at the reception desk and also assuring them that she'd be back in the morning with her mother to discuss further arrangements.

***

It was around 2 a.m. when they arrived back at the club, by which time everyone else had gone home. Carlito lived there, of course, and as he did every night, he was busy tidying up before shutting up.

Carlito was a large man in his early sixties, with a bushy beard. He paused in checking his accounts and gave them a concerned look.

"How is Mario?" he asked.

Adriana sighed. "The surgery went well. Something is still wrong though, but they haven't said what it is yet. I have to go to the hospital with mama in the morning for an explanation."

Carlito sighed too and stroked his bearded chin. "So long as he isn't going to the morgue like Renato, it can't be that bad."

"Where are the police?" Gabriel asked as he walked past the bar towards the bandstand.

"The police have come and gone. They wanted to question Adriana, but none of us knew which hospital you'd gone too. So, they'll be back sometime tomorrow afternoon to speak to us all again." He made a disgusted gesture towards the dancefloor, which was still garish with its smearing of Mario and Renato's blood. "Until then, I'm ordered to leave the floor exactly like that. They say it may jog our memories as to exactly what happened."

Which statement Adriana understood to mean that, just as expected, nobody present during the shooting had admitted to seeing anything.

"Why were they in such a hurry to leave?" she asked.

Carlito shook his head. "I don't know. I overhead one of the detectives mention Joao's name, so maybe they got a tip elsewhere that it was he who'd done the shooting. Anyway, they left as if they were in a hurry to catch a thief."

"I hope they do catch him," Adriana said. "He's not safe to be on the streets. He should be behind bars."

And then Gabriel drove her home to give her mother the bad news of that night's happenings.

CHAPTER 4

"We can count on most of the people in Casa de Carlito tonight to keep their mouths shut," David Luiz told his companions when they reached his house. "They all know better than to mess with us."

Joao nodded. The first thing his friends had done once they'd arrived at David's small apartment was to forced several cups of coffee down his throat. The coffee had shaved the edge off of Joao's drunkenness—he still felt in an elevated state of mind, but not as bad as it might have been if the caffeine hadn't been working against the alcohol in his system.

David's apartment was small, but the building was a quiet one. At the moment, Joao and David sat in opposite chairs in the living room, while Pedro was off rummaging about in David's kitchen.

"You got any booze in here?" Pedro asked, suddenly reemerging from the kitchen with disappointment etched on his handsome face. "I need a damn drink. We fled the club so suddenly I didn't even finish my whiskey."

"There'll be no more drinking tonight," David Luiz said, speaking Portuguese in clipped flat tones. "If Joao here had been drinking less, we'd not be in this goddamned mess now."

David Luiz was dark and thickset, and along with Joao, shared the leadership role in their gang, *As Cobras Negras*. No one, not even Joao, argued with David Luiz when he looked the way he now did, which was as moody as hell, as if he and not Joao had been the one who'd shot Renato. Pedro was tall and skinny, very good-looking, and was generally easy-going. Age-wise, all three gangsters were in their early thirties.

"Don't look that damn serious," Joao told David. "Renato had it coming to him. I was gonna have it out with him sooner or later."

David shook his head. "Hey, I already told you to leave Jane alone. This town is full of pretty ladies and everyone knows that Jane is in love with Renato."

Joao laughed. "Not anymore. She needs to fall in love with someone else quickly."

David stared angrily at Joao, then he shook his head. "You need to sober up quickly. The police are now after you for murder. Your shooting that Fernandez kid doesn't help matters either. We'd better hope the kid doesn't die, or that will be two murders the cops want you for."

Joao understood David's anger and frame of mind. He and his gang brothers were all one and the same. None of them saw the least thing wrong with his killing Renato Barbosa. Renato had done similarly to members of rival gangs. This was common knowledge and simply the life they lived in the criminal underworld they inhabited. No, what had David irked was the public nature of Renato's slaying. Joao losing control of himself like that and shooting Renato Barbosa in the front of a crowded club was the problem, because it would now focus the attention of the police on their criminal activities, amongst which were drug smuggling, gun-running and organized prostitution.

"Hey, relax, David," Pedro said, after having resigned himself to the man's insistence on no further drinking tonight. You know as well as I do that no one at the club will dare finger Joao. Definitely not with Mario Gomes and the rest of our guys and girls remaining there tonight to tell us who did so."

"You're forgetting that the kid Joao shot knows very well who shot him," David Luiz retorted. "And his sister does too. And even if those two don't squeal to the cops, we've still got Carlito himself to consider. Carlito is good friends with Renato and his gang."

Joao nodded to this. David was speaking the truth. It was well known in Casa de Carlito that Carlito only tolerated their presence there. True, *As Cobras Negras* were arguably the most influential gang in downtown Belém, but Carlito had been a gangster himself in his younger days and he still had some influence. Carlito was close friends with José Martins, father of José Martins Junior, the leader of *Os Vermelhos*—the other main gang faction who frequented his bar, which had been the now-deceased Renato's own gang. Because of this Carlito was very partial to *Os Vermelhos*.

Joao mused over this point. *The main reason Carlito hasn't kicked us out of his bar is because he is scared that doing so would place him in a position where Os Vermelhos can then order him around and even extort him. With us there a balance of power will be maintained.*

"At the moment, Carlito isn't the problem," David said. "What we need to worry about now is where to hide Joao so that the police don't find him." He stared from Joao to Pedro and back again. "My suggestion is that you hide here, until we discover which way the wind is blowing."

Joao shook his head. "Ah, I don't know, David. How safe is this place?"

David smirked. "Ah, you're sobering up at last; that's the first sensible thing you've said since arriving here."

"Yeah," Pedro said, taking a seat opposite the television, with a nervous look on his face. "How safe is this place? The police could show up here at any moment."

David waved their worries away. "Don't sweat it. Remember that I just moved here. Even my own mother doesn't yet know where I live." He frowned at Joao. "So long as you keep your head down and don't make a nuisance of yourself with any of the single ladies in the other apartments in the building, you'll be safe here."

Joao nodded and that decided it. "Yeah, I'll stay here for the time being. I'll keep out of sight until we figure things out."

CHAPTER 5

Gabriel had called to say he would pick Adriana and her mother up that morning. He arrived while they were eating breakfast. While neither woman had any actual taste for food, Bruna Fernandez had insisted that they eat something before setting out for the hospital.

"We have no idea how long we'll be there," she wisely pointed out. "We may be there all day long."

Gabriel hadn't eaten any breakfast himself and joined them for a cup of coffee. And then the trio set off for the hospital in Gabriel's van.

While they rode, Adriana peeked into the back of the vehicle, looking for last night's bloodstains. To her relief, Gabriel had washed them out of the van. She felt a surge of gratitude to him for doing that; his kindness and consideration were two of the primary reasons that she liked him so much. She simply couldn't imagine what her mother's reaction would have been if she'd looked into the rear of the van (which wasn't screened off from the driver's section) and seen all that blood.

***

Adriana recalled the events of the previous night after Gabriel had dropped her off at home. Gabriel had wanted to come inside too, but she'd asked him not to. Her reason was a simple one. Even though the time then had been almost 3 a.m., it was certain that once her mother heard what had happened to Mario, she would want to immediately set out for the hospital, where she would insist on sitting until daybreak.

And if Gabriel's van was still parked outside their house, Adriana would likely find it impossible to dissuade her from doing so.

She'd explained as much to Gabriel, who had nodded that he understood, hugged her, and then driven off into the night.

Adriana had then entered their little home alone. Bruna Fernandez had been fast asleep after a hard day's labor. It had seemed such a shame to wake her up. Because of Mario's dream of attending medical school, their mother been doing more work than she should have and saving the money.

For a few moments, Adriana considered letting her mother sleep till morning, before she broke the bad news to her. But she felt too restless to fall asleep herself and knew that except she had company of some kind, she'd go half-crazy from apprehension before morning.

So, she had woken her mother up, and told her what had happened. But first, she took the precaution of both taking off her bloodstained jacket and of also washing Mario's blood off her hands.

Then, she'd been very careful in exactly how she presented the news to her mother. To start with, she'd told Bruna that Mario was in hospital but wasn't in danger, and then, between bursts of tears, she had explained what had happened at the club.

In retrospect, Adriana realized that it had been a good thing her mother had been asleep when she'd gotten home and had needed to be awakened as this had meant that Bruna had at first been too tired to fully comprehend exactly what her daughter was telling her, and as such be overwhelmed by the bad news. By the time the sleep had properly cleared from her eyes, Adriana had gotten around to telling her mother that Mario's operation had been a success and that he was out of danger, and so Bruna herself was forced to accept the bad situation with relative calm.

However, just as Adriana had foreseen, Bruna's relative calmness on receiving the bad news didn't prevent her from wanting to leave at once for the hospital. Nor did the fact that the hospital in question was quite a distance away deter her either. Adriana had to forcibly restrain her mother from leaving the house at 4 a.m. and looking for a late-night taxi to get there.

"You should have called me from the hospital," Bruna kept reproaching her, to which all her daughter could reply was, "Mama, let's just be grateful that Mario is fine now."

"Fine? If he's fine, what does the doctor want to see me for?"

"I've no idea. Relax, mama, we'll both find out in the morning. Now go back to bed and try to get some sleep." This was stated in vain. She knew that her mother wouldn't sleep a wink till morning.

But Adriana herself needed to rest. Once she'd gotten fresh reassurance from Bruna that she wouldn't dash out of the house once left alone, Adriana had staggered off to bed, where, no matter how hard the excitement of the night tried to keep her awake, her eyes soon shut.

***

Now, seated between Gabriel and her daughter in the front of the van. Bruna kept blinking tears away from her eyes as Gabriel drove them to the hospital.

Adriana kept quiet and smiled as encouragingly as she could each time her mother glanced at her.

Gabriel reached the hospital and parked in the front parking lot. He couldn't see the doctor with them as he had to drive to his part-time job, which was doing graphic design as a printer's assistant.

"Call me once you're done here, and I'll pick you up," he told Adriana through the van window after she and her mother had gotten out of the vehicle.

"Thank you, Gabriel. You're a good boy," Bruna Fernandez said, while looking nervously from the parking lot towards the front entrance of the hospital, and flinching while two men dashed past her, carrying an empty stretcher towards a parked ambulance.

"Won't returning here be too stressful for you?" Adriana asked Gabriel, though she felt grateful that he cared so much. "Yesterday, you were saying how your boss was after you to finish designing those new political posters."

Gabriel shook his head. "No problem. I have to take the day off anyway. Remember that Carlito said the police want to see us at the club this afternoon."

His statement brought the horrible memory of the club's still unwiped bloody floor to Adriana's mind and she winced before replying: "Dammit, I'd forgotten all about that. Okay, Gabriel, I'll call you."

Gabriel nodded and drove off.

***

This morning Doctor Sanchez seemed less harried than last night. (In contrast to Adriana's friend and crush Gabriel who was slim and almost borderline anorexic, the surgeon was rather plump, though also tall.)

They saw him in his office, where he gestured them both to seats.

"Thank you for operating on my son and saving his life last night," Bruna told the doctor with tears brimming in her eyes. "I really don't know what I'd have done if you hadn't been able to save him." Then she looked confused. "But what do you want to see us about?"

"If it's about the bill, we'll do our best to pay it promptly," Adriana said hurriedly.

The doctor shook his head. "No, it's not about that—though Mario does require certain medication that we don't stock here, and which you'll need to purchase from the pharmacy. No, what I need to talk to you both about is the effect of the bullet on his life."

On those words, Adriana felt a choking feeling in her chest, like a giant hand was squeezing her rib cage. Her mind immediately filled up with a million questions, none of which she could ask right then, as the doctor was still speaking.

". . . Unfortunately, the bullet struck Mario in the lower part of the spine, completely severing his spinal column in the lower lumbar region. To cut a long story short, he's paralyzed from the waist down."

"Paralyzed?" Adriana stared incredulously at the doctor. "Are you serious? Mario is paralyzed?"

She turned to stare at her mother. "Mama, did you hear . . . ?" She stopped. Bruna's mouth was wide open, and she looked utterly horrified, no words emerging from her shocked face.

"I'm very sorry, but that's the truth," Dr. Sanchez said gently. "Mrs. Fernandez, your son Mario will never walk again. He will be stuck in a wheelchair for the rest of his life."

Adriana could only stare from the doctor to her mother and back again. Now she too was too horrified to say anything.

***

Dr. Sanchez led them to Mario's ward. Mario's bed was one of eight in the ward. He was hooked up to several machines, and when they arrived at his bedside, a young nurse was taking his temperature with a digital thermometer.

"You can speak to him for a short while—not more than five minutes," Dr. Sanchez whispered to them at the foot of Mario's bed. "He's too medicated to really communicate with you both, but he knows that both of his legs are paralyzed and is understandably very upset about that." The doctor nodded to them both. "I'll be in my office when you're finished speaking to him. Then I'll explain to you the special needs of someone in his condition."

"Thank you, doctor," Bruna said, while Adriana nodded.

Adriana watched the doctor leave the ward and then she and her mother waited while the nurse attending to Mario gave him an injection. Then they both walked towards the head of the bed and stood beside him.

Mario stared up at them, with a mixture of worry and confusion in his eyes. Like Dr. Sanchez had told them, he was drugged up against the pain and appeared to be fighting to remain awake, because his eyes seemed to continually lose focus. But one thing was very clear to Adriana; her younger brother was very distressed and in a state of intense mental torment.

All of this is because of that crazy fool Joao Ramires, she thought with intense anger.

Bruna was bending over Mario and stroking his brow. "It's alright, son," she told him. "Everything will be alright."

"Mama, I can't feel my legs," Mario said in a miserable voice. "Mama . . . Addy . . . I can't feel my legs anymore. Where have they gone to?"

Adriana began crying as she stood there by the bed.

"It'll be okay, son," Bruna kept telling Mario. "Just you get better and leave the hospital. Mama will take care of you. Everything will be okay, Mario."

But Adriana really doubted anything would ever be alright again.

***

"Paralyzed?" Gabriel asked, with a confused look on his face.

"That's what the doctor says," Adriana sadly replied. "Mama is so distraught, she's in shock. And me? For the past twelve hours I've been living in a nightmare wishing someone would wake me up."

As agreed, Adriana had phoned Gabriel after she and her mother had spoken to Dr. Sanchez again. Most of their discussion with Dr. Sanchez concerned things she'd expected once the doctor had earlier informed them of Mario's condition: the need to get him a wheelchair, lots of vitamins and other medications, and most important of all, the need to provide him with a loving support system. "At the moment he most likely feels like his life is over. It's important that you emphasize the positive aspects of his situation, which is that he is still alive, and that many people in his condition are still able to live fulfilling lives, so long as they accept the reality of their situations."

Adriana agreed with Dr. Sanchez, but that didn't make her feel any better. After speaking to the doctor, Bruna had returned to Mario's bedside, and had refused to leave there even when Gabriel had arrived to pick them both up. So finally, they'd left her in the hospital, with Gabriel promising to return for her after their meeting with the police.

Adriana still felt mad at Joao Ramires for causing she and her family so much trouble. After her initial sure of rage, was now remained was a slow-burning resentment of the man that threatened to boil over at the slightest provocation.

"I hope the cops find him quickly," she told Gabriel as he drove them through the city.

Gabriel nodded. "Me too. I can't forget how Renato looked dead on the dancefloor."

***

When they arrived at Casa de Carlito, the others were all waiting. Daniel and Lucas (the two band members who had accompanied them to the hospital last night), Carlito, and both Jane and her best friend Maria.

Along with two police detectives, everyone was arranged around two tables near the dancefloor. Both of the band members had beers in front of them. The others, including the two officers of the law, didn't. Adriana and Gabriel were pointed to empty seats at the table.

The detectives investigating the shooting incident were named Lopes and Wagner. Lopes was a small, bearded man, while Wagner was larger and clean-shaven. Both were middle-aged and were dressed in crumpled gray suits and were sweating in the afternoon heat.

Adriana formed the immediate impression that these two detectives were crooked cops. She of course had no proof that this was the actual case, but just at this moment, she was in a bitter frame of mind and ready to think the worst of anyone.

Making matters worse for her was the wide red splash on the dancefloor. Illuminated in afternoon sunlight streaming in through the club's opened windows, she found it shocking to see so much blood, as if a large hog had been slaughtered on the dancefloor. The blood was dried up now, but that fact didn't in the least lessen the impact of seeing it.

Once she and Gabriel were both seated at the table with the detectives, Carlito introduced her as the elder sister of the other shooting victim. Both detectives nodded their greetings to her.

"How is your brother now?" Detective Wagner asked. "It took us a while to discover that he is at Mercy Hospital, not Saint Jude's like the guitar player told us last night. The young man must've been very stoned for him to mislead us so badly."

Adriana told them Mario's condition.

"That's very bad," the detective said. "Very bad indeed."

"Forgive us for bringing the seven of you here like this," Detective Lopes said next, while looking from one face to the next. "but we have two crimes on our hands and a startling lack of witnesses to what happened."

"This strikes us both as very odd, and very sad too," Detective Wagner added in a sour voice. "One would naturally expect that in such a crowded place as this, at least one person would know who shot Renato, and"—he pointed at Adriana—"this young lady's brother as well."

His companion nodded. "Actually, we already know who shot both people. But we need corroborative evidence." The detective sighed loudly. "Unfortunately, too, no one present last night had the presence of mind to film the incident. They only seemed to realize this was something newsworthy afterwards, as represented by the many photos posted online, all of which show only the aftermath of the shooting, not the actual event."

"So, who shot them?" Maria asked. Maria was a small and pretty woman who was known to be very fond of club owner Carlito. In fact, judging from how close she was sitting to Carlito, Adriana decided the two of them had now begun dating.

"We know Joao Ramires did the shooting." Detective Lopes went on. "We have one witness who saw the incident and is willing to testify in court." He sighed. "But one witness isn't enough. All of you know that Joao is part of the *As Cobras Negras* gang, and that all of their members who were present here last night will be willing to swear that Joao didn't shoot Renato, and possibly even finger our own witness as the murderer."

"So, we need more witnesses to the shooting," Detective Wagner added, wagging a finger in the air to emphasize his point. "You can rest assured that your identities will be kept secret until the trial commences—and hopefully beyond then too."

"As you'll have noticed, we're not revealing the identity of even our current witness," Detective Lopes said. "There's too much possibility that someone might want to ensure they don't make it to court to testify."

Detective Wagner nodded.

Adriana nodded too. Her thoughts were muddled. On the one hand, now that she was past last night's fiery rage over her brother's injury, she shared the caution of the others at the table, none of whom had so far ventured to speak. But on the other hand, whether by accident or design, she didn't know which, she was seated in such a way that looking straight ahead meant she was looking between Carlito and Detective Wagner, and behind and between them lay the unmopped stain of blood. That stain really worried her, it wasn't so much the sight of it, as the knowledge that the man who'd created it out of two other people was still at large, and (knowing how gang members generally behaved) was probably even boasting about it right now to some woman.

"Now, we can't force any of you to speak," Detective Wagner said softly. "And if you don't agree to testify in court, we won't think any less of any of you. But still, we're asking you all to reconsider your statements." While saying this, he focused his gaze primarily on Carlito, Jane, and Maria. Then he looked at the musicians too. "My partner and I asked you four to meet us here this afternoon, because you're the ones who took the wounded kid to the hospital. None of you have made any statements yet. So now we're asking you too: did any of you see what happened?"

"I didn't," Lucas promptly replied. He gestured back over at the stage. "Man, I'm the drummer. I'm behind everyone so I really can't see what's happening out on the dancefloor."

The detectives nodded and looked at Daniel, who also shook his head. "Me, neither. I heard the shots but thought it was another amp malfunction." He laughed softly. "Okay, I'll admit I was a bit stoned too, so my perspective can't be considered reliable. I actually thought my bass amp had blown up again." He pointed across to the stage. "It's that big thing over there, like two boxes stacked on each other. When it blows up, you'll think someone's shot me dead."

The detectives nodded again, their eyes now looking disappointed.

"I saw the problem starting," Gabriel said. "But I'd looked away when the shooting happened."

The detectives sighed and looked at Adriana.

She felt their eyes piercing her like spears. She knew she was their last chance to put Joao Ramires behind bars. *If I also say I didn't see anything last night, the case will be dead, Joao will get off scot-free . . . and then he'll most likely shoot someone else in another club at some point in the future.* She also became aware that, aside from the investigators, all of her companions around the table were mentally willing her to deny witnessing the incident too. But then she looked between Carlito and Detective Wagner, through to that red patch on the floor, and her resolve to do something firmed in her heart. *Yes, last night I agreed to not say anything; but that depended on Mario being okay.* She felt tears coming to her eyes again. *Oh, but now Mario is far from okay! No, Joao can't get away with doing this to my family. He must pay for what he has done.*

She smiled at the two detectives, both of whom were still watching her quietly. She recognized the look of expectation on their face and hoped that she was about doing the right thing.

"I saw everything that happened, and I'm willing to testify," she told the detectives. "I was sitting at my piano at the edge of the stage; and so, yes I saw everything clearly."

Oddly, her words brought loud sighs of relief from around the table. She looked at her friends. No one seemed critical of her decision. Even Gabriel nodded at her.

Both detectives nodded also, and then Detective Wagner brought out a digital audio recorder from his pocket and switched it on.

"Go on and tell us what happened," he said. "We'll record your statement and have it typed out. Then, afterwards, you can read through it and sign it."

Detective Lopes smiled at Adriana. "You're a very brave woman, Ms. Fernandez. Trust us, we'll do all we can to keep you anonymous."

"You know, I think I too remember what happened last night," Carlito said, just as Adriana was about to begin recording her statement. "Yeah, I did see Joao Ramires shoot Renato and Mario."

"I did too," Maria said immediately afterwards. "I was right there beside the three of them and I saw everything that happened."

Detectives Lopes and Wagner nodded and then looked at Jane, who hurriedly, and with a very nervous look in her eyes, shook her head.

"I didn't . . . I mean . . . I wasn't—" she began stuttering, before Maria came to her rescue and finished for her: "Trust me, she didn't see anything. Jane was gesturing over at our table, trying to get someone to come pull Renato away before trouble started."

Jane gave her friend a grateful look; one that the detectives apparently didn't notice.

"So, now we have four witnesses," Detective Lopes said with satisfaction. "Let's get you three all recorded. Once your story matches that of our other witness, Joao Ramires won't have a hope in hell of escaping a long, long jail sentence."

"Make that *five* witnesses," Adriana corrected. "You're forgetting my brother Mario. He was there and saw exactly what happened. I'm certain he'll want to testify in court if it helps put Joao behind bars."

As Adriana told her tale to the detectives and their audio recorder, she felt good about what she was doing. It felt like she was lifting a heavy weight off her chest. She was certain she was doing a major public service by getting that thug Joao Ramires off of the streets of Belém.

Once the two detectives had left the club, Carlito got out a mop and began working on the bloodstained dancefloor. He had to get the place clean before the club patrons began arriving for the night's revelry.

CHAPTER 6

By that evening, the news of the club shooting was all over town. Joao Ramires had become an infamous celebrity.

"I can't believe this nonsense is happening to me," he told David angrily, when the latter returned from a visit to his father's auto workshop. "Each time I turn on the news, I see myself. It's like I'm now the only criminal in Brazil."

David sighed and dropped his bag on the coffee table. "Well, at least you're famous now."

Joao stared at David Luiz in anger. He was unsure if David was making fun of him or not. "I still cannot believe that someone dared to finger me to the police. When I find out who did it, I'll . . ."

David didn't appear to notice his anger and shrugged back at him. "I'm as surprised as you that anyone dared to rat on a member of *As Cobras Negras*, the most feared gang in all of this state. Still, Joao, you're lucky the Fernandez boy didn't kick the bucket. All the police want you for now is killing Renato."

"That is bad enough," Joao said sullenly.

David shook his head. "It's not as bad as you think. You know how our police behave. If you lie low long enough, something bigger than Renato's death is bound to come up and then, witnesses or no witnesses, the police will forget all about you." He handed over a packet of fast food to Joao. "For the moment, you can still go out at night—but only in disguise. It's good that you and Pedro are about the same size. So long as we stay away from Casa de Carlito, everyone will simply mistake you for him." He sat down beside Joao and studied his friend for a moment, reaching out to stir Joao's long hair back and forth, until finally Joao swatted his hand away, and asked:

"What's with all the touching? You turning gay, or what?"

David laughed. "I'm thinking you'll need to cut your hair short like Pedro's. That'll heighten the illusion that you're him."

Joao nodded his agreement. Disguising himself was very good thinking. He was looking forward to hitting some of their gang's old haunts again.

"I'm tired of hiding," he told David honestly.

David laughed again and forked tortilla chips into his mouth. "It's only been two days. Much too early for you to be tired."

But yes, Joao really was tired of hiding. Although he had only been hanging out at David's apartment for two days, he was already bored to death. It seemed incredible to him that he, the great Joao Ramires (Joao had inflated ideas about his own importance in the scheme of life) was now a fugitive.

All he could do here was either watch TV or read, and since he wasn't much on reading, television it was then, daytime soaps and samba musicals. At first Joao had tried to follow developments in his case on social media, but Pedro had rightly pointed out that the police could easily track his cellphone. On David's request, he'd handed the phone over and according the Pedro, the cellphone now safely resided somewhere at the bottom of the Acará River.

So, both yesterday and today, Joao Ramires had watched TV until he thought his newly force-fed mass media knowledge about the intricacies of contemporary Brazil was about driving him mad.

David's other request (actually it was more of a rule), was that Joao refrain from drinking while he was hiding here. At least, not when he was alone in the apartment.

"Hey, they're burying Renato on Friday," David said.

"I'd love to be there and spit on his coffin," Joao said. "That son-of-a-bitch is the reason I'm in this mess."

"Just don't attempt it," David said with narrowed eyes. He spoke with a worried look on his face, because he knew Joao was crazy enough to do exactly that—attend Renato Barbosa's funeral and attempt to dishonor the man even after murdering him.

But then Joao laughed and nudged David with his elbow. "Don't worry. I've already sent Renato to hell. I'll let him arrive there in peace."

On hearing this, David heaved a loud sigh of relief. "Okay, so just lay low here for a couple days more. Tomorrow, I'll have one of the girls—maybe Hilda, since she once worked in a beauty salon—come give you a haircut."

"Yeah, yeah, whatever," Joao agreed with a dismissive wave of his beer can. "Hey, has Dominic supplied us with that stash of weed yet? I need a hit, I'm almost going crazy."

"Nah, Mario Gomes says Dominic says the cops are hanging around his place, like they suspect you'll get in contact with him."

Joao sighed. Surely it couldn't get any worse than this.

***

Joao's safe house at David's out-of-the-way apartment lasted until the next day.

At about noon the next day, Joao ran out of cigarettes. This lack was particularly unfortunate because there was nothing else in the house by way of recreational drugs. With the current police heat on *As Cobras Negras* since Joao shot Renato, the plan was to move all of the gang's narcotics operations over here to David's new apartment, but David's car (which was built with secret compartments for drug and gun smuggling) had suddenly developed engine trouble, meaning the intended transfer of drugs had to be put off.

So there was no cocaine or marijuana in the apartment, nothing to take the edge off of Joao's boredom as he watched soap opera after soap opera and commercial after commercial. He had no cellphone, no internet, and once more began feeling like he was going crazy. (His only other distraction was to imagine himself brutally punishing whoever had given his name to the police. The person's name hadn't been released to the press, and as such wasn't in the news, but Joao found great satisfaction in imagining himself throttling the fool to death.)

David had said he'd bring them some marijuana in the evening, along with some girls for a party, but evening was still six hours off and Joao found himself becoming increasingly antsy as time dragged endlessly on.

And so it was, that at about two-thirty, Joao Ramires decided to sneak out of the apartment to buy himself some cigarettes and a six-pack of beer.

Yes, he realized that the beer drinking by himself would be against David's rules, but who the hell was David to tell him what to do anyway? He and David Luiz had formed the gang together, and David Luiz owed Joao his life—Joao had even gotten knifed for him once. So who was David Luiz to start dictating to him on what or what not to drink, and when or when not to imbibe it?

After examining himself in the bathroom mirror, Joao set out for the supermarket up the road, at the highway junction.

When he stepped out of house, it began raining and Joao mused that the elements were favoring him. *God must be pleased with me for getting rid of that son-of-a-bitch Renato Barbosa for him. Or, if not exactly pleased, at least he's not too angry with me for shooting the Fernandez boy.*

He considered going back up to David's apartment for an umbrella, but decided to brave the rain as it was. The rain was little more than a drizzle and Joao figured that even if it increased in intensity, he'd have made it to the supermarket before he got drenched.

By way of camouflage, he was wearing a hoodie and dark glasses. On examining his reflection before leaving the house, he'd been concerned that he'd be recognized, but the hoodie seemed a good disguise, particularly once he pulled it down really low, so his face was mostly hidden. He didn't think looking like this would raise any alarms; nowadays, lots of urban youth dressed this way. And besides, most people should logically assume the hood was down so low because of the rain.

Joao reached the highway, looked left and right for policemen, and then, seeing none, slipped into the supermarket.

Once inside the building he asked a clerk for the Alcohol and Tobacco section of the supermarket. The young woman answered him without the slightest hesitation. Joao observed that she didn't seem too concerned about how low his hood covered his face. *That's good,* he thought.

Joao looked up over the nearest shelves, at the customers shopping about, and then, dropping his head again, he headed in the direction the attendant had indicated. Yeah, she clearly saw nothing wrong with his dressing. To her, he was merely another customer.

He relaxed. *It's silly to expect all the police in Belém to be looking for me,* he thought, taking the cigarettes he wanted from the rack. *This town has lots of crime, and to be honest with myself, I'm merely small fr—*

That was when he noticed the two policemen who were peering in at him from the window. Worse still, was the little old woman standing beside them, who was gesturing at him and nodding her head fiercely. Joao didn't recognize the old woman, but he could read her lips as the police listened to her.

"He's the one I saw on TV—that nasty Ramires hoodlum who shot the kid," the old lady was saying. "No doubt about it. I immediately recognized his face when he looked up at the ceiling after entering the supermarket."

Joao panicked. He almost didn't know when he began running for the rear of the supermarket, looking for an exit.

And that was how Joao Ramirez was apprehended by the Belém police and wound up in jail.

CHAPTER 7

"I can't believe it," Adriana told her mother, Bruna, in disbelief a week later as they both watched the evening news on the small TV in their apartment. "They've caught Joao Ramires and now they're letting him go again?"

The TV screen showed, as a large inset on the newscaster's left, Joao Ramires leaving the court in company of his lawyer, a fat black man with a thick mustache and a beaming smile.

Adriana's mother sighed and looked away from the TV, instead letting her gaze rove around their dingy apartment, taking in the depressing details of this place that marked their poverty: the dirty old wallpaper, the faded window drapes, the old chairs, and the cracked and scratched coffee table. And then she peered through the kitchen door at the ancient and grimy counter, on which lay the desolate thawing chicken that would be tonight's dinner.

Mario was still in hospital, and the old woman felt sad; she felt incredibly sad for her son. Because, for Mario, his dreams seemed to have ended, his once bright future punctured and drained away by a gunshot. All of the money the family had been saving for his college tuition had gone into covering his hospital bills; in addition to which both Adriana and Bruna had borrowed still more money from friends and relatives.

With that act of senseless violence, the Fernandez family hadn't just fallen back to square one. They had dropped below the default setting for poverty and were now desperately trying to haul themselves up to a perch of equal lack with their neighbors.

At the moment, Adriana kept an eagle-eye watch on her mother to ensure that Bruna Fernandez didn't relapse into depression and start drinking again like she'd done after her husband had died.

Bruna felt equally sad for herself and sad for Adriana too. For how long would their poverty and misery continue?

But at the moment, Adriana was almost beside herself with rage. "They're giving Joao bail? And they've pushed back his trial by six months? What if he flees the country?"

(When Adriana had initially told her mother of her intention to testify against Joao Ramires, Bruna had been scared of gang reprisals. But she had grudgingly agreed once Adriana told her the police were keeping all of the witnesses' names a secret.)

Bruna Fernandez frowned at her daughter. "Listen, child, you know that's the way things are here. This is nothing new." While saying this, she crossed herself and said a silent prayer for herself and her daughter. She looked at the TV again, where thankfully, the image of the criminal who'd shot and paralyzed her son Mario had been replaced by other bad news.

Bruna very well understood her daughter's rage. Mario's shooting—with all of her son's hopes being brutally dashed to pieces—seemed as senseless as an elephant angrily stamping on a butterfly.

When Bruna once more addressed Adriana, her voice was soft and calm, her sadness again packed away in her soul.

"We have bigger problems now than the lousy government," she told Adriana, pointing at the brand new wheelchair over in the corner. "Your brother Mario will never walk again. We need to remain positive, and help him accept his terrible loss when he leaves the hospital."

Adriana stared back at her mother and began to cry. "Oh, mama, why is our life so hard?"

Her mother got up and went over to her and hugged her. "We do the best we can, my child," she said with tears in her eyes also. "We can only do what we can."

CHAPTER 8

Adriana was relieved to be spared more unpleasant discussion with her mother, because their conversation was interrupted by the loud blaring of the horn of Gabriel's van. He honked twice and on the second blast of the horn, Adriana leapt to her feet, and quickly dried the tears from her eyes.

"You're going out again?" her mother asked.

"We've playing tonight at the Paradise Club," Adriana replied.

She kissed her mother on the cheek and left the house. She looked forward to seeing Gabriel tonight. Being with him always cheered her up. She was wondering how soon it would be before he asked her out on a date and they became lovers. She knew the reason he'd not yet said anything was because of her current family situation. He seemed to have been gathering up his courage to date her and then—Bang!—right out of the blue, the whole Renato/Joao/Mario incident had occurred and put a damper on things.

Still, they were good friends. That was a good start.

Outside, however, Adriana's pleased anticipation that she'd be riding alone with Gabriel in his van was dashed. Once she got close to the van she saw he already had a female passenger.

"Hi," Vanessa Carlos hailed her, expelling cigar smoke as she reached the white vehicle. Vanessa was their band's new singer. A sultry brunette with a voice to melt one's heart. She was beautiful too. Adriana was wary of her; Vanessa had already shown signs that she liked Gabriel a little too much. Meeting her here in Gabriel's van now was a glaring indication that she was trying to get as close as possible to him.

"Hi, Vany," Adriana greeted Vanessa. "But, what are you doing around here? I thought you lived on the other side of Belém, closer to tonight's gig."

Vanessa shrugged and exhaled some more cigarette smoke, while opening the door of the van so Adriana could get in beside her. "My older brother works near Casa de Carlito," she explained dismissively while scooting sideways towards Gabriel. "I came over to see him, found that he'd gone out and decided to drop in on Gabriel instead."

Adriana got into the van. Vanessa's excuse sounded dodgy at best. *Why come all this way to meet with your brother without first making a cellphone call to find out if he's available to see you?* At least that was what Adriana would do in a similar situation. She decided Vanessa had simply needed an excuse to come see Gabriel.

But that was neither here nor there. For the moment, while Gabriel drove the van away from her house and up her street, Adriana forced any worries about romantic competition from the singer from her mind and concentrated on mentally preparing herself for the night's gig. She looked into the back of the van and saw that Gabriel and Vanessa had already collected their musical instruments from Casa de Carlito; so at least Vanessa turning up had saved her the effort of loading up her keyboard and amplifier.

A Latino-rock band was billed to perform at Carlito's tonight so they wouldn't be missed.

***

Tonight's venue, the Paradise Club, was a drinking and dancing venue twice as large as Casa de Carlito; in addition to which it was situated closer to the richer part of Belém, and thus catered to a wealthier clientele.

When Gabriel, Adriana, and Vanessa arrived at the Paradise Club, the place was half-full, with more clubbers arriving all the while.

The rest of the band were waiting for them, setting up the stage, and ensuring everything was in order. In the meantime, people drank their beers and wine to the accompaniment of a DJ.

A phone call from inside the van on their arrival meant that band guitarist Joey was waiting to help unload the remaining equipment from the van. This consisted of Adriana's keyboard and amplifier, Daniel's bass amplifier (which was too big to take away from Casa de Carlito unless it was essentially needed elsewhere), and a box of cables and auxiliary equipment, stuff like spare microphones, extension sockets, and duct tape.

This final set of equipment was carried/wheeled through the club's side entrance and quickly set up.

And then, after being introduced to the American couple who ran the Paradise Club, it was time to play. The band filed on stage, and the emcee unclipped a microphone from its stand.

"Ladies and gentlemen, the Paradise Club is pleased to present to you the band Sistema de Música!"

There was loud applause as the emcee left the stage. Adriana looked around at everyone, Lucas on drums, Joey and Daniel on guitar and bass respectively, Gabriel on trumpet, and Vanessa handling most of the vocals. Yes, they really were a good combo, one that Adriana thought had potential.

Lucas counted in the beat for the first song, which was a version of *Cuida Bem Dela*, and they began playing.

At first, Adriana felt some stage fright. This was always the case at a new venue when one played for the first time to an unfamiliar audience. Their residency audience at Casa de Carlito knew each of them personally and would easily cut them some slack if they gave a bad performance, but here in a place like this, it was a different story.

Most of the audience here had never heard them play before or even heard of them, and so they had to be won over; they had to be turned from mere bystanders and spectators into ardent fans of Sistema de Música.

That was the weight of apprehension that Adriana Fernandez felt as she looked out into the Paradise Club's affluent, well-dressed audience while she and her companions played. The faces looking back at her were expectant and it was soon clear to her that they liked what they were hearing. This automatically communicated itself to the entire band, who now all relaxed and did what they did best—put on a hot jazz and samba show.

Now that she felt secure in the glow of the audience's acceptance, Adriana relaxed and gave herself to the music. As the concert progressed, she felt like she was transcending herself and fusing with the music, becoming one with it, letting it take control of her and play itself out to the world through the medium of her body, through the agency of her fingers. At times, particularly when she was playing duets with either Gabriel or Daniel, and also when she and Gabriel backed Vanessa Carlos on *The Girl From Ipanema*, it really felt as if she were a tool in the hand of a divine power.

At those times, her face seemed to glow, and she felt magic communicating itself both to the band and to the audience.

In a short while, the audience was all up and dancing; the dancefloor filled up. On seeing this, Adriana felt a burst of apprehension, as if she expected history to repeat itself. But then she relaxed again. This was a more uptown joint and a classy place; thugs—gangster riff-raff like *Os Vermelhos* and *As Cobras Negras* —would never be welcome in here.

Finally, it was over. The band had been playing nonstop for two and a half hours, songs, solos, and improvisations, all of which the audience lapped up like a pack of thirsty dogs at a stream. To loud applause, the band did an encore, and that was it.

Afterward, while they sat around a table, chugged soft drinks and beer, and ate snacks provided by the club, Gabriel gave them the good news:

"Guys, we've been offered a second residency here. Twice a week, and the pay is . . ."

Adriana listened with a delighted feeling. Combined with what they already earned from their primary residency at Casa de Carlito, the amount the Paradise Club was offering them meant she'd have enough to finish paying off Mario's hospital bills and also make some improvements to their poor home.

Remembering her mother's sad tears before she'd left home, Adriana said a silent prayer of thanks to the Almighty. At the moment, things were definitely looking up for her and her family.

CHAPTER 9

Once out on bail, Joao didn't waste much time before holding a meeting with David Luiz and Pedro. The rest of the gang weren't invited because, as David said, the less people in the know the better.

The first item discussed was how Joao's lawyer and bail money had eaten deeply into the gang's profits.

"We used most of our money for the lawyer and your bail," Pedro explained. "David had everyone working overtime to make up what we needed."

"I know that," Joao said in a dismissive tone of voice. "We'll make more money." This wasn't his first taste of jail, and now that he was back at David's place, he vowed, just like he had several times before, to never be a guest of the police again. Brazilian police weren't civilized like those in the western world. His body still ached from several beatings.

Joao was also surprised by how high-profile his case had become. Maybe because there wasn't anything else really newsworthy happening at the moment, the local press were playing up how he'd brutally paralyzed the Fernandez boy, putting him in a wheelchair for life.

Somehow, the sob-story angle made Joao look even worse than shooting Renato did.

Renato Barbosa's death was widely viewed as one hoodlum killing another; nothing to get excited about. But the Mario Fernandez shooting was viewed differently. Reporters had discovered that the kid had been working at the club to save up money to go to medical school, and now there was a huge outpouring of emotion at Joao for having ruined the kid's dream of becoming a doctor.

They're going to throw the book at me once I get into court, Joao realized. It was an alarming thought for him, one that had often played through his mind while he'd been in jail, before his bail had been granted. Brazil didn't have the death penalty, but the lawyer had told him he was staring at the maximum permitted sentence—life in jail; possibly, to keep the public happy, two parallel running terms.

David waved his right index finger at Joao, and shook his head. "Yes, we will make more money, but not to waste on that fat lawyer again." He smiled coldly. "We need the money for ourselves."

"Hey, what are you talking about?" Joao instantly protested. "I need that money to have a fair trial. I don't want to go back to prison."

"And you won't," David promised. "But to ensure that you don't go to prison, we need to eliminate all the witnesses to the crime you committed."

Pedro, who had been standing by the hallway door, and hadn't really contributed to their conversation, now crossed the living room to the couch and sat down opposite the others. Then he said: "The lawyer has already told David and I that you've no chance of beating the rap. Too many witnesses saw you shoot Renato and the kid. Even if the prosecution plays down Mario's killing as being accidental, the fact is that you shot him while intending to shoot Renato again—that's a murder attempt. And the witnesses—"

"Yeah, the damned witnesses," Joao angrily interrupted. "Next time I'm gonna kill someone, I'll ensure there's no one watching me."

Pedro pulled out a joint from a shirt pocket and lit up. "That's the spirit. We can start by killing the witnesses like David suggests."

"Too many of them," Joao pointed out, reaching out a hand for the joint after Pedro had taken a long drag on it. "No way we can knock off everyone who was in Casa de Carlito that night." He inhaled the narcotic smoke and sighed. "I still can't believe those club patrons weren't too scared to rat on a member of *As Cobras Negras.*"

David shook his head. "We don't need to worry about killing everyone, just five people."

Joao perked up at that info. He exhaled marijuana smoke into the room and looked inquiringly at his two friends and partners-in-crime. "Just five witnesses? How'd you arrive at that small number? I remember that there were almost fifty people in the club that night."

David Luiz shook his head when Joao offered him the joint. He was always like that; tried to keep a clear head for business. "The lawyer told us," he explained. "He paid a police contact of his for the information. And I confirmed it myself through a cop friend of mine. You know the guy—Bento. Everyone else told the police they saw nothing that night."

Joao nodded. "Those are the smart ones. Who are the foolish five?"

"Just everyone we expected," Pedro replied. "Carlito, Renato's younger brother Tomás, the Fernandez kid and his older sister Adriana, and—"

"And of course, Renato's girlfriend Jane," Joao finished for him. "She must be dying to put me behind bars for decades for killing the love of her life."

Joao was surprised when Pedro and David both shook their heads.

"No, Jane isn't saying a thing. When the police questioned her, she said she was looking away from the men when it happened and didn't see anything."

"Smart woman," Joao said through a cloud of smoke. "I always thought she was smarter than Renato and this proves it." Then his brow furrowed. "So, if Jane isn't the last snitch, who is?"

David smirked. "It's her friend Maria, the one who was beside her at the club that night."

Joao's confusion showed on his face. "Maria? But what does it have to do her? I know she didn't like Renato. And I have no business with her either. So why does she make trouble for me?"

Pedro sighed. "That's women for you, Joao. We found out that Maria began dating Carlito just before the shooting."

"Maria will surely regret letting that old fool influence her against me like this," Joao said angrily. He saw now that David was looking at him questioningly.

"So what do you think?" David asked. "Do you agree that we eliminate them all and, by so doing, both prevent you from going to prison and also save ourselves some money in legal fees?"

"Yeah," Pedro pointed out. "Without witnesses, the prosecution doesn't have a case. And with no case against you, we don't need the lawyer."

Joao smiled, feeling a surge of confidence for the first time since he'd set the ball rolling on this mad dance by killing Renato. "Yes, I agree completely that we rid ourselves of the snitches."

David finally accepted the joint from Pedro. He took a hit of marijuana and then the three men huddled together to finalize their deadly plans.

CHAPTER 10

At the Sistema de Música rehearsal, everyone's spirits were very high because of their second residency at the Paradise Club.

Carlito wasn't initially pleased to discover that he was now sharing his house band with the more uptown venue and grumbled darkly about finding another music group to take over the Casa de Carlito residency, but Adriana and Gabriel had come prepared for this reaction.

Adriana sweetly pointed out to Carlito that the band's new residency was a win-win situation for both of them.

The giant club owner instantly disagreed with her. While the band waited for Lucas and Vanessa to arrive for the rehearsal, Adriana and Gabriel were seated at the bar opposite Carlito, who was taking inventory and polishing drinking glasses.

"Win-win?" he asked, squinting at her. "Ah, Addy, what do *I* win by giving up my best band for part of the week?"

He gestured over at the performance stage, where Daniel was tuning his bass and Joey was watching something on his cell phone and laughing. "I treat you all like my own family, like my own children even. I give you all a nice place to rehearse and play, and today, you come here and stab a poor old man in the back and steal my customers away to another and bigger club."

"Ah, Carlito, don't be like this," Adriana said. "We only play here three nights a week, and the Paradise Club gigs will only be on Wednesdays and Saturdays. You usually have a DJ on those days anyway."

"And the Saturday Paradise gig starts at 10 p.m. So if you want, we can play here first before heading over there," Gabriel added.

With one hairy and brawny arm placed on the bar between them, Carlito ruminated on this, but he still looked displeased, so Gabriel explained further: "What Addy meant by a win-win situation for all of us, is that the money Sistema de Música makes from the other residency will enable us buy better equipment to use here too."

"Lots of new and more modern musical instruments," Adriana quickly added, though she knew she was stretching the truth a little, because in her case at least, all of her extra earnings would be swallowed up by bills at home. And she knew Gabriel was several weeks late with his house rent again and his landlady was on the verge of evicting him, so he was unlikely to be replacing his old trumpet any time soon. The same also applied to both Lucas and Daniel; each of whom had waiting bills of their own to tend to. Just like herself, Lucas was the primary breadwinner for his family, while Daniel's wife was expecting another baby, which meant a third young mouth for their family to feed.

But Carlito was unlikely to care about any of that, and it was important to protect the band's residency here at Casa de Carlito, because even though Carlito paid them peanuts most of the time, here was a good place to practice, being roughly central to the distances each of them had to commute from either work or home to get here.

So Adriana went on: "And better equipment means we will sound better on stage when we play here, which means many more customers for you and more money for everyone."

"Yeah, old man," Gabriel agreed, and then pointed meaningfully at Carlito. "And then you can give us that raise we've been deserving for over a year now."

Carlito smirked and scratched his beard. "Nonsense. I already pay you lot better than anyone else would." Like most businessmen, he disliked talking about parting with money, and Gabriel's suggestion that they might want more money had subtly shifted their discussion to placing him on the defensive. So, to end this disturbing trend, Carlito smiled crookedly at the two young musicians.

"Okay, we'll see how it goes for a while. But if I'm not satisfied with the results—"

"Hey, darling!" At that moment Maria poked her head around the side of the stairwell at the far left end of the bar, causing a broad smile to immediately replace Carlito's negotiating frown.

"Yes, darling, what is the matter?" he replied her.

Maria waved at Adriana and Gabriel. "Nothing, Carlito, but can you come upstairs for a minute? I need your help with something."

Adriana waved back. Inwardly, she was very surprised. So Maria had moved in with Carlito now. She decided it didn't matter. Carlito was a widower, and Maria had made no bones about the fact that she desired to be his woman.

"We will talk more later," Carlito hurriedly told Adriana and Gabriel, and left them at the bar.

"That went better than we expected," Gabriel said when Carlito had vanished upstairs.

"Yeah," Adriana agreed. "It was a genius idea for you to mention that we wanted a raise over what he already pays us for playing here."

Gabriel laughed softly. "Yes, that scared him, didn't it?" His laugher died. "Hey, Addy, how's your brother doing? I haven't had time recently to visit him in the hospital."

She sighed. "He's alright, I think. At least, as well as can be, given the circumstances. You know like I said it's gonna be hard for him to—"

Vanessa and Lucas arrived then. Lucas waved to them and walked past the bar towards the stage, to attend to his drum kit.

Vanessa, however, joined them at the bar.

"Hi, guys!" She nodded to Adriana, and then kissed Gabriel on the cheek. Then she made a point of remaining close by Gabriel's side. "What's been happening today?" she asked.

Adriana shrugged. "Not much, but we've gotten Carlito's grudging approval of our Paradise Club residency." She realized that she felt very uncomfortable seeing Vanessa standing that close to Gabriel, who disturbingly, didn't seem to mind. Adriana figured it was either that

Gabriel was oblivious to Vanessa's seductive charms, or that the pair of them had already begun dating; though she didn't think the latter option was the case. Vanessa still seemed rather desperate to be noticed by Gabriel. She wasn't taking the kind of liberties with Gabriel that a girlfriend would, like stroking his hair, or fiddling with his clothes. Even her kiss on his cheek had been chaste, hinting of desire, but still almost sisterly. Adriana realized that Vanessa's standing so close to Gabriel was designed to stake her claim to him; to warn other young women—meaning herself, Adriana—to keep away.

She concealed a smile. *Sorry, Vany, but he's not yours; he's mine. It's just a matter of time till he and I get together.*

Which made her wonder what still delayed them professing their liking for each other. A worry formed in her mind, that if she wasn't careful, Gabriel might soon think she wasn't interested in him and switch his emotional allegiance to their band's singer.

"Where's Carlito?" Vanessa asked. "I need a Coke."

Gabriel grinned. "He's upstairs . . . most likely making love to Maria."

That brought smiles all around. Then, Vanessa pointed to the stage. "You were right, Gabriel, the stage at the Paradise Club will do much better for the new band videos."

Gabriel nodded.

"What are you two talking about?" Adriana asked, her eyes narrowing slightly. "What new band videos?" It bothered her that they'd been talking about band stuff behind her back.

"Oh, you know Vanessa is in film school," Gabriel explained. "She's suggesting that it's time we updated our current YouTube videos with a fresh set."

Adriana looked at Vanessa for confirmation.

Vanessa nodded back. "Yes, it's true. What you've got uploaded now looks so dated—not fresh, not modern at all. And the location where they were recorded? So old and lackluster; almost dingy."

"Hey, lower your voice," Adriana urgently whispered to her. "Most of those vids were shot here, and Carlito is very proud of them. And if he hears you badmouthing the look of his club, we'll all be out on our ears, without a rehearsal space."

Vanessa's eyes widened, and her next statement was a whisper too. "Okay, okay. What I'm saying is, I can bring a student film crew over to one of our gigs at the Paradise Club and record the band performing there. That way we'll have something a lot more professional on our YouTube channel and our other social media and music streaming websites." She sighed dramatically. "I don't know about you guys, but I don't intend being an unknown forever."

"It's a good idea," Gabriel said. "What do you think, Addy?"

"I think it's a great idea," Adriana conceded gracefully, though it hurt her to admit it. Because doing so meant admitting that Vanessa had brains as well as beauty, which made her more of a romantic threat. It was also annoying to realize that the other girl's ambition and fledging film industry connections meant she might be able to do more for their band than Adriana herself had so managed, although this wasn't just *her* problem. The entire Sistema de Música band had been working hard to break out big-time for ages, without success.

"And it's not just the video recording I've got in mind," Vanessa said enthusiastically. Then she looked around to see if anyone was emerging from the stairwell.

Gabriel shook his head and laughed. "Don't worry your head about the old man. As old as Carlito is, sex with Maria would be like taking valium—a knockout punch. Don't expect him to resurface before we're done rehearsing."

"We'd better get started on rehearsing," Adriana said after a look at her watch. "I told mama I'd keep Mario company this evening while she attends mass."

They walked towards the stage, with Vanessa continuing her speech. "Okay, so another thing I'm thinking is . . . One of the girls at the film school, Lucia, has a brother who's a radio DJ. She might be able to get him to play some of our songs on his radio show, but we need to get some good quality recordings. Either studio recordings or, a live recording that's really high quality, so we'll need to—"

Adrianna nodded along with Vanessa's ideas, but her mind was no longer with her companions. Her distraction had occurred when they'd been crossing the dancefloor, specifically when they'd walked past the spot where Mario and Renato had been shot. The ground here was of worn old tiles, and because, by instruction of the police, the dancefloor hadn't been promptly cleaned on the night of the shooting, its stone covering was now slightly stained, the blood having penetrated into the cracks and crevices and become adhered to the stone. This resulted in an effect like what resulted if one spilled coffee on a different-colored rug. Even after cleaning, a discolored patch might still remain as a faint reminder of what had happened.

And so it was in this case also. The discoloration on the stones wasn't a major one, but it was obvious to anyone who knew what had happened here and paid attention, like Adriana always did, to that portion of the dancehall floor.

Each time Adriana saw that part of the floor, bad emotions surged through her; just like they did now.

She wasn't alone in disliking the faint patina of blood. Carlito hated it too. The club owner had done his best with his mop to get rid of it, but hadn't succeeded.

(The reason Carlito disliked the bloodstain was because seeing it was a constant reminder to him of the upcoming trial at which he was testifying. He'd told Adriana that he often felt nervous about agreeing to testify, with her reply to him being that she felt nervous too, but that so far she saw nothing to indicate that any of them were in danger. Detectives Wagner and Lopes had kept true to their word: none of the witnesses' identities had been released to the public.)

Carlito's proposed solution now was to paint over the floor at that point with a large red star, with the words Casa de Carlito boldly emblazoned around it, so that the concealment masqueraded as part of the club's décor. But he claimed he didn't have enough money yet to afford either the paint or the painter.

So, in the meantime, that part of the floor continually distracted Adriana Fernandez. Twice she'd told Gabriel, that sometimes she felt so bad on seeing that discolored patch that she considered quitting their band.

By the time she and the others joined the rest of Sistema de Música onstage, she realized she'd not heard anything Vanessa had said. Vanessa's question as to what she thought about her promotional ideas, all of which seemed to have met Gabriel's unreserved approval, was replied with a slight nod and "Cool, we'll discuss it later." Vanessa seemed pleased enough with that and walked away from Adriana to test her microphone.

"Hey, can you put a little more reverb on my voice?" she asked, while Adriana turned on her portable Yamaha synth and selected her favorite electric piano patch.

They began rehearsing, starting with a new samba song that Vanessa had brought them, and Adriana let the music take her to its special, secret places.

With no dancers in the club, she found her attention riveted to the bloodstained floor. Once more she felt a triggering of horrible memories. At first, she felt in control of herself, but all of a sudden the horrible feelings rose to such a violent crescendo in her soul that it was all she could do to refrain from weeping. She played on, trusting her soul to the music, trusting to the music to save her from her terrors. It was all she could do, otherwise, she would leap up from her keyboard screaming and run out of Casa de Carlito, never to return again.

"Wow, you're fantastic!" Vanessa said after that number. I've heard lots of people play the piano, but you're something special."

"Thanks," Adriana smiled back at her. Once again the music had saved her; she felt composed now; the patch on the floor was once more merely a stain and not the summation of her inexpressible fears. She regarded Vanessa calmly. Now that she was in the musical flow, she felt too elated to diminish herself with petty romantic rivalry, or her suspicion of Vanessa's motives, which to a degree looked like she wished to take over control of their band.

"You're a fantastic singer yourself," she in turn complimented the other woman.

Vanessa sighed. "This is really a great band we've got here. I just hope we can make it big. It'll take a lot of work, but I'm a real workhorse."

Adriana felt herself warming even more to Vanessa. "We'll see. Maybe fate will smile on us."

They resumed rehearsing. Thirty minutes later Carlito and Maria came downstairs, which provoked much laughter from the band.

Adriana laughed too at the embarrassment on the lovers' faces.

CHAPTER 11

Late the next night, Joao, David, and Pedro sneaked back along the same alleys which, a month ago, they had fled down.

The time was 2 a.m. in the morning and the three men were headed back towards Casa de Carlito. They had arrived here in a borrowed car, which they had left parked about a block away from their point of entry into the clumped array of buildings that formed this downtrodden section of Belém City.

In contrast to their previous trip down this strip of alleys between the buildings, tonight, Joao, David, and Pedro moved as silently as cats stalking mice. Even though they were in a hurry, their haste didn't make them incautious.

The majority of the windows they passed were unlit and were it not for the fact of their caution, they might have reached their destination in a third of the time it actually took them to arrive there.

When they got to Casa de Carlito, the last of the club musicians were just leaving.

"I thought they weren't playing tonight," Joao said as the three of them crouched in the shadows of the store next door to the club.

"No, no, that was last night," Pedro whispered back.

The night was hot around them, the heat adding an instinctive irritation to their anticipation of the dark deed they were here for.

"What concerns us is that they're leaving on schedule," David Luiz pointed out to the others. "We couldn't come yesterday because we heard Maria had gone to visit her sister. Had we come here yesterday, we'd have missed Maria. But tonight . . ."

With the assistance of both band guitarists, the band leader was loading several amplifiers into the back of his van. While watching them with slitted cold eyes, David pulled out his knife and waved it at the others, taking care so that it didn't reflect the lights from the club windows at the departing musicians.

"It is too bad that the Fernandez bitch quit working here after her brother got shot," Joao said, while pulling out his own knife and testing its razor-sharp edge against his right thumbnail. "Or else, tonight we could have killed three birds with one stone; not just two."

David grunted. "That would have been too complicated. It's much better this way. We can take care of her later."

So, they crouched in the shadows waiting until the band had all loaded themselves into their van and had driven away. Then they waited to ensure that no one else was coming out of the club.

Then, before Carlito would have a chance to lock up for the night, they crossed to the club entrance and slipped inside.

"You wait here at the door," Joao instructed Pedro. "Remember, only shoot if there is no other option."

Pedro nodded and pulled out his gun. "Of course, of course. This must be done silently."

With that agreed on, David and Joao walked through the empty foyer into the club proper.

Carlito was at the bar, tidying up before retiring for the night. The club owner was preoccupied with estimating the contents of the bottles of liquor on the shelves behind the bar and so didn't notice them enter. The radio at the end of the bar played soft samba music. Half of the lights were turned off, and the chairs had all been upended onto the tables to make the floor easier to mop in the morning. Both the stage for the musicians and the dancehall area were darker patches within the general dimness of the building's interior. Silence now prevailed where barely an hour ago raucous noise and jubilation had held court. The smell of people lingered in here even now, when the revelers and dancers had all departed for their beds.

"Maria isn't with him," Joao whispered to David, pulling him back into concealment behind the door. "Our information was wrong."

David scratched behind his ear. "No, Maria must be here. She'll join Carlito in a short while. If she doesn't, it means she's gone to bed early."

Joao nodded and waved his knife at David. "I'll go and confront Carlito. You keep an eye out for Maria."

But David shook his head. "No, let's do it the other way. If Carlito sees you, he'll instantly suspect something is up and react accordingly. But he's not seen me here since your arrest, so he won't know what I'm here to do." David gestured across the bar with his knife. "You just keep your eyes peeled in case Maria suddenly comes down the stairs, or else she will wake up the entire neighborhood with her loud voice."

"Okay," Joao reluctantly agreed and remained out of sight behind the door. Still, he simmered with disappointment that he would not be the one killing Carlito. Just like David, he felt the burning desire to brutally harm the two witnesses.

He grunted impatiently as David made his way across the bar to confront Carlito. David had his knife concealed behind his back so that Carlito wouldn't see it, but Carlito was now staring at his ledgers anyway and after a long shift and a few glasses of rum was apparently oblivious to the world until David tapped him on the elbow.

Then Carlito looked up in surprise, although his surprise suddenly turned to distaste and irritation. "You? Boy, what the hell you doing in my bar? You know very well that I don't have time for you anymore. That goes for your gang of ruffians also."

Carlito pulled himself up to this full height, which meant that he now towered over David Luiz. But then, as anger filled him, he leaned forward over the bar, so that he could reproach the younger and smaller man face-to-face, which once more brought them both to the same height.

"Calm down, old man. I'm not here to fight. I just want to—"

"You and that idiot Joao Ramires turned my club into an unsafe place, and now the police keep on sniffing around, claiming they're looking for drugs and whatnot. I—"

"Hey, old man, Joao says he's sorry. He did not mean to shoot Renato that night—"

But Carlito wasn't interested in listening. He seemed to grow angrier by the moment and, what was more worrisome to both David Luiz and Joao, his voice was getting louder: "Listen, I have no interest in what you want to say. Tell that fool Joao that he can go t—"

Carlito never saw the knife coming. Still leaning over the table so he could vent his anger at David, all he knew was that something cold and razor sharp had entered his neck. Then there was intense pain as the cold object was jerked sideways across his throat.

Carlito staggered back and looked down at himself. The blood was gushing from his throat like water from a tap opened to its fullest.

He gaped at David in disbelief.

David waved the bloody knife at him. "You go to hell first, old man."

"Maria! Maria!" Carlito gasped, as he steadied himself with one hand on the bar, trying not to fall down and enter that final darkness. His other hand tried futilely to stop his neck from bleeding. Maria's name emerged like a frog's croak from Carlito's bloody lips. He was trying to scream out a warning to his lover, but the blood and his severed windpipe made it impossible for him to attain the necessary volume.

While keeping an eye on Maria's possible emergence points into the club, Joao quickly walked over to the bar and smiled at the dying man.

"See you in hell, Carlito."

Carlito's feet gave out beneath him then and he slumped down out of sight behind the bar.

Joao nodded at David. "Good job. Now let's go take care of Maria. She must be sleeping upstairs."

***

As they walked towards the staircase, Pedro appeared at the door. He said nothing, just stared at them with a question in his eyes.

64

"So far, so good," David told him. "Just the girl left now."

Pedro vanished back to his watch post and the other two ascended the stairs.

It took them a short while to find Carlito's bedroom, but once they did, the rest was easy.

Maria was asleep in bed, her slumbering form illuminated by dimmed lighting that reflected off of her blue nightgown.

"I will be the one who silences this bitch," Joao whispered once they'd stepped inside the bedroom.

"She is all yours," David agreed.

As Joao Ramirez approached the sleeping woman, he was consumed by a sudden desire to make a real example out of her, to make her feel a lot of pain as she died.

With this in mind, he walked around the bed till he was level with her shoulders and then knelt on it. Next, he clamped his hand tightly over Maria's mouth and stabbed her hard and deep in the belly. He loved the look on her face when she jerked awake in both agony and confusion, and he relished her accompanying horror when she realized what was happening and also realized that tonight she had no escape from death and that none of this would have happened to her if she had kept her big mouth shut.

Joao laughed as she began thrashing about. When Maria got over her initial shock and tried to feel the wounds in her belly, Joao smacked her hands away from her body. Then he stabbed her again, even more violently.

"Hey, take care not to get her blood on your clothes," David Luiz cautioned Joao.

"That's okay," Joao replied. "They're still clean."

Maria was already dead. Though she was still staring at Joao, the life had gone out of her eyes.

Joao nodded over to David. "Okay, the loudmouth puta can no longer testify against me in court. We can leave here now."

***

David and Joao hurried downstairs to join Pedro at the front entrance of the club. As they passed through the main room with the bar and dancehall, Joao gestured over towards the darkened stage where the band usually played.

"Just the musician, her brother, and Renato's brother to take care of now," he said.

David nodded his agreement and they slipped outside. Shortly afterwards, the three men were making their furtive way back the way they'd come, maintaining the utmost silence, until they reached their borrowed car and drove away.

All in all, they considered it a good night's work.

Killing the remaining three witnesses should be just as easy.

CHAPTER 12

Adriana felt a heavy depression settling on her as she and her brother sat in their living room. Their mother was out of the house at the moment, visiting friends. She herself had just finished a lengthy practice session on her portable Yamaha keyboard and now felt like relaxing with a soap opera. But once she recalled today's news about Carlito and Maria, relaxation seemed impossible.

She was however glad to have Mario back home again, even if he was now sitting in his wheelchair instead of a normal chair. Him being here made a lot of difference, compared to having to visit him in hospital.

Mario seemed to be bearing up well. At times his depression was obvious, but he had chosen to make the most of a bad thing; particularly because in this case at least, his dark cloud really did have a silver lining. Because of the publicity his misfortune had received in the media, several of Brazil's top universities had offered him scholarships to study in their medical schools, so long as he could pass the entrance examinations.

"I still can't believe what happened to Carlito and Maria last night," Mario said.

Adriana didn't really want to discuss the club owner and his girlfriend's grisly deaths, but she knew there was no avoiding it. "Neither can I," she told her brother. "You know that Sistema de Música rehearsed at his club yesterday, and both he and Maria seemed very happy together. That's the more reason this news of their violent deaths shocks me so much. Sure, I heard rumors that Carlito was dealing marijuana and some cocaine, but no one I ever spoke to thought he was big-time, at least not big-time enough to warrant getting killed like that."

Mario nodded and aimed the remote control at the TV, changing the channel. "Yeah, I thought he was small-time too. But the cops found lots of drugs at his place. They're saying Carlito must have pissed off one of the big cartels, possibly the Columbians or the Mexicans. They're the ones who get bloody like this."

Adriana grimaced. "This is all the more reason why we need to put violent hoodlums like Joao Ramires behind bars where they can't hurt the innocent." She noticed her brother's grip on the remote control tighten, his fingers whitening, as she went on. "And finally, there's some good news for us: Mama told me they've changed the judge who's hearing Joao's case."

"Huh?" Mario looked at her.

Adriana nodded. "Yeah, it's true. They're suspecting Judge Soares of ethics violations. They've apparently been investigating him on suspicion of accepting bribes to pervert justice for a while now."

Mario frowned. "Who are they replacing him with? Another corrupt man?"

Adriana shook her head. "No. I don't remember the new man's name, but I hear he wants to make an example of Joao." She shrugged. "Mama says he's looking for the death penalty for Joao."

Mario shrugged back. "It won't work. Everyone knows that nowadays in Brazil, you only get the death penalty for terrorism and war crimes, not for everyday hooliganism, even if it includes murder. The highest penalty for those is life in jail."

Adriana shook her head again, more emphatically this time. "But that's the thing, Mario. According to mama, this new judge on Joao's case wants to pursue a *domestic terrorism* charge against him, to make an example of such egregious behavior in public places such as bars and clubs."

Mario looked doubtful. "I guess it might work, but Joao's gonna be mad. In a way it's unfair to him, isn't it? I mean, adjusting the punishment *after* the crime has been committed?"

"I don't see how that should concern you," Adriana coldly replied her brother. "He's not the one who is currently stuck in a wheelchair— you are. And if nothing is done about him and his like, we will just keep having more innocent victims like yourself. Just look at what's already happened to both Carlito and Maria, both of them witnesses in your own shooting case. As far as I'm concerned, I'll be happy if Joao gets the death penalty, so long as it gets him out of our hair."

Mario's lips tightened as he accepted his sister's argument.

After a pregnant pause, Adriana added: "And who's to say even, that maybe Joao Ramires didn't put the cartels up to killing Carlito and Maria, just to get them out of the way so they don't testify against him?"

No more was said on the matter after that. Brother and sister resumed watching TV, where a hilarious family comedy had just begun showing, a program that successfully, for a time at least, soothed their differing worries.

However, neither of them was aware that knowledge of this latest legal twist in the case against him had merely firmed Joao's resolve to kill *them*, so that they didn't help the law kill *him*.

CHAPTER 13

The next night was Lucas's birthday. He was twenty-five that day and the band were having a party for him at Gabriel's apartment, which was quite spacious.

Adriana attended the party. Gabriel had invited Mario along too, but Mario said he couldn't make it because he needed to study for his upcoming medical school entrance examinations. Mario then confided in Adriana that he'd have loved to attend Lucas' party, but he was still too nervous to visit anyone.

Adriana assured him that she understood his reservations. She told him not to worry; that in time, he'd regain his social confidence.

So Adriana went to the party alone. Actually (though she took great pains not to show it), she was relieved that her brother wasn't accompanying her. This wasn't because she was in any way ashamed of Mario, but because tonight she had something to take care of; something that might take quite a bit of time to resolve; and she wouldn't be able to concentrate on seeing to that matter if she had to watch out for Mario at the same time.

Her intention tonight was simple: Adriana had decided that, with Mario now home from the hospital and in a positive state of mind, she had no reason to continue to overlook her potential relationship with Gabriel.

Yes, she told herself as she ascended the stairs to Gabriel's third floor apartment. *I have to take care of this tonight.*

Her plan was a simple and direct one. After having a few drinks for courage, she would pull Gabriel off to a quiet spot somewhere. (It was, after all, Lucas's birthday, not Gabriel's; and so, even though the event was happening at his place, he shouldn't be in such high demand as to be missed if he left everyone for thirty minutes.) Once Adriana had Gabriel all to herself, she intended to none-too-subtly demand that he and she discuss their forever-on-the-horizon romance, and decide whether or not they were actually going to start dating.

Adriana figured that once she gave Gabriel that much of a push in the right direction, the rest of it would take care of itself. That would be that; she would finally have a boyfriend, and the competition from sultry Vanessa, who seemed to be worming her way closer and closer to the bandleader day by day, would be over.

She thought that taking the initiative like this was a good plan, and one that was certain to succeed. Their matters of the heart would be resolved tonight, for sure.

She rang the buzzer and Gabriel's younger sister Chloe let her in. The large apartment was filled with young people who were lounging, drinking, and dancing. Music was being provided by one of Gabriel's DJ friends, a long-haired, long-bearded fellow, whose eyes showed he was already spaced out on pot. The air held a thick smell of marijuana and sweat from all the dancing happening.

A quick survey of the living room showed Adriana that most of the band were present. In the improvised dance area on her left, the birthday boy Lucas was dancing with a gorgeous blonde girl that Adriana didn't recognize, while on her right Daniel's heavily pregnant wife Lucia was lounging with her back up on pillows. Lucia noticed Adriana and waved to her.

Adriana waved back and then returned her focus to Chloe, who'd just let the band's guitarist Joey and his girlfriend Katie into the apartment.

"Hey, where's your brother?" Adriana asked Chloe.

Chloe and Katie were kissing cheeks, after which Chloe took a moment to shut the door behind the new arrivals. Then she grinned at Adriana. "Gabe? Oh, he was in the kitchen. I think he went in there with Vany."

Chloe turned and hurried off through the partiers.

A couple near Adriana stepped out onto the dancefloor and locked lips with one another. The sight of them kissing filled Adriana with a feeling of urgency. Having been here several times before, she was familiar with the layout of Gabriel's apartment. The kitchen Vanessa and Gabriel had supposedly entered was at the far end of the living room, but there were too many dancers in the way for her to see across to it. So she made her way across the room, ducking around the gyrating bodies as the DJ changed the samba track he'd been playing to a hot EDM number, and whoever was controlling the lights dimmed them a bit.

Adriana finally made it through to the hallway which led off to the kitchen.

This short corridor was also filled with people, most of whom were dancing with bottles of beer and plastic cups of wine in hand, while others were entering and exiting the bathroom at the far end of the hallway.

Adriana glanced down the hallway and steeled herself. *I need to do this,* she told herself, *placing her hand on the kitchen door. If Gabriel is talking to Vany, I'll ask her to excuse us for a short while.*

However, just as she was about to open the door, it burst open and Gabriel's sister Chloe emerged from in there giggling.

"Hey, get a bed, both of you!" she yelled back into the kitchen.

"Get lost, brat!" came the laughing reply in a familiar voice.

Adriana froze while Chloe slammed the door behind her. She had the dismayed understanding that she'd just stumbled on something she'd rather not have.

Chloe, bottle of wine in hand, was still laughing. "Hey, Addy, you don't want to go in there now," she said, tapping the kitchen door with an index finger. She then lowered her voice to a conspiratorial whisper. "Gabe and Vany are in there kissing."

"Kissing?" Adriana was forced to ask.

Chloe, who'd already drank too much alcohol to realize the implications of what she was revealing, nodded emphatically, obviously mistaking Adriana's surprise for amusement. "Yeah, they're kissing. I don't even think Vany has any panties on." She giggled. "I can't really blame my brother though. He and Vany just began dating yesterday—do you know she spent the night here? They made so much noise I didn't get any sleep." She slipped her free arm through Adriana's. "Hey, come with me," she said and began tugging her away from the kitchen door.

Adriana let herself be pulled away. She felt deflated, as if all of her willpower had suddenly drained out of her.

Gabriel and Vanessa became lovers just yesterday? Oh, my God, no!

She accepted the cup of wine Chloe poured for her, and then sipped on it while her mind struggled to come to terms with what had just happened, how she had just lost the guy she wanted to date to Vanessa, who had apparently not had the same qualms as herself about waiting for the right time to let him know she was available for romance.

Chloe and her boyfriend (Adriana could never remember the kid's name) were talking to her, but she couldn't understand what they were saying. It wasn't just her own mental haze of disbelief that was blocking out their conversation; the EDM was almost too loud to hear herself think.

She finished her cup of wine and held out the cup to Chloe for a refill, which was promptly provided. Adriana then left the two of them and headed across the room, looking for Lucas, so she could give him his birthday present—a rare 'Live in Brazil' CD by the great American trumpeter Fats Walker.

She found Lucas, handed him his present and wished him a happy birthday, and then wondered what to do with herself. Her surprise at the discovery she'd just made had ironically anesthetized her against its own effects. Full-blown disappointment had not yet set in; she merely felt numb.

She felt like leaving the party, but realized that doing so would look suspicious. Chloe, for one, would instantly deduce why she'd departed the party so quickly.

I'll have to endure the party for a while; until I can reasonably excuse myself and leave for home. And I'll need to wait till I see Gabriel before leaving, so it doesn't look like I'm resentful of his preferring Vanessa to myself and I'm running off to mope. Whatever happens, I need to be classy about this.

She looked around for someone to talk to. Most of the party attendees were currently dancing, so she moseyed along till she reached Daniel's wife Lucia, who was maybe the only person at the party not currently shaking to the latest hit by Lady Gaga.

"Hey, how you doing?" Lucia shouted above the music as Adriana sat down.

"Oh, I'm good," Adriana lied back above the music. Then to make conversation, she pointed to Lucia's swollen belly. "How's the newest addition to the Pinheiro family coming along?"

Lucia smiled proudly. "You mean *additions*. We're having twins."

"Twins?" Adriana's face reflected her surprise. "But you already have two kids."

Lucia nodded and laughed. "Yeah, that's why Daniel is so pleased you guys got that new regular gig at the Paradise Club. The money is really gonna help."

Their conversation went smoothly after that.

Somehow, Gabriel and Vanessa never showed up in the living room. It was either they had spent the whole party kissing in the kitchen, or they'd retired to one of the bedrooms so they'd have more privacy.

Adriana, meanwhile, made the best of a bad situation. She gave Lucia her full attention and by the end of that evening was quite the expert on modern Brazilian antenatal procedures.

Then she went home and cried herself to sleep.

CHAPTER 14

Two evenings later, which was Sunday evening, Mario and Adriana went shopping.

This was Mario's first excursion out of the house in his wheelchair, and Adriana wanted to make it special for him, to fill him with a sense of anticipation as to the good things life still held for him despite his disability.

She herself also needed to leave the house. The memory of how she'd lost Gabriel to Vanessa still hurt her badly. She felt very sad and yet she knew she needed to be very strong now, particularly because of her brother. She saw no point in preaching positivity to Mario, while she herself was gloomy. So, she did her best to put Vanessa and Gabriel out of her mind, and she concentrated all of her energies on making her brother feel happy.

Sunday being what it usually was, there was very little traffic about as they made the short walk. The road was also free of pedestrians. Most people were just waking up from long afternoon naps taken to dodge the sweltering heat, and still wouldn't be out of doors for a while yet.

"So how ready do you feel?" Adriana asked as she pushed Mario's wheelchair along the sidewalk.

"I'm confident I'll pass, though I wish I had a few more days to brush up on my biology," came the cheerful reply.

Mario was in a good mood. He was due to take a special entrance exam for the UFMG College of Medicine, which was based down south in Belo Horizonte, that Wednesday and had been studying as hard as he could to be ready. It was during a break from his endless reading that Adriana had suggested that he accompany her to the nearby market.

"Sure, I'd love to be accepted at UFMG," Mario continued. "But I'd really prefer somewhere closer to home, where I'd be able to visit you and mama from time to time."

"Oh, don't worry about that," Adriana said encouragingly. "Even if you're over in far-off Belo Horizonte, I'll make sure to come visit you often. I may even relocate, not that mama will ever allow that."

"And you, Adriana, what do you plan on doing now?" Mario asked, looking back at her.

She smiled, pleased by the happy look on his face. "Well, first of all, let's get you settled down and accepted into medical school. Then, once we're sure what your immediate future holds—"

"Hey, why's that crazy guy driving like that?" Mario suddenly asked, pointing ahead of them into the street.

And that was when Adriana noticed that a white car which had just turned the corner ahead, had veered off the opposite lane and was headed for them, weaving from side to side as it crossed the road. From where Adriana stood, both men in the vehicle seemed to be wearing dark sunshades and baseball caps.

She waited a moment to see if the driver would get control of the car again, but when he didn't, she realized that the car driver might be drunk and that both she and Mario were in danger of being run over.

Oh no! Adriana did several quick mental calculations, and then, as the time to impact dangerously shortened, she began trying to get Mario's wheelchair out of the way.

CHAPTER 15

The white car speeding towards Adriana and Mario was a stolen Honda Accord being driven by David Luiz, with Pedro riding shotgun.

To avoid rousing the suspicions of the police that they were the ones behind all the deaths of the witnesses, Joao and his two friends had decided to stage the Fernandez siblings' exit from this life as a hit-and-run road accident by a drunk driver.

They had been cruising back and forth past the Fernandez house for an hour now, waiting for their chance to strike, and now they had apparently hit pay dirt.

Joao himself wasn't in the car. His absence from the crime scene was considered essential, and besides, Joao had deadly business of his own to handle tonight.

In case someone did later identify either David and Pedro (although they thought their very basic disguises sufficient proof against this happening), both men were also slightly drunk, and had empty beer cans inside their stolen ride. By their criminal reasoning, if the police stopped David and Pedro afterwards, the best case the state could present against them would be ones of car theft/drunk driving.

But meanwhile, their deadly car was almost on Adriana and Mario.

"Get them both before she gets away!" Pedro yelled at David when he noticed that Adriana was pushing Mario's wheelchair out into the street, which would mean they would miss hitting it.

"They aren't getting away from us!" David said grimly, both stomping on the accelerator while speaking, and at the same time, also twisting the steering to adjust the trajectory of the car so that it would catch both siblings even if Adriana did successfully launch the wheelchair towards the relative safety of the middle of the road.

But David's compensation proved to be unnecessary. Either because she panicked when he altered the car's direction, or because she was simply too confused to begin with, or because one of the wheels of the wheelchair snagged on something on the pavement, Mario's elder sister was unable to put his wheelchair in motion.

She however kept trying, right up until the last moment, when her self-preservation instinct kicked in and she flung herself sideways into a clump of bushes.

Her action saved her, but not Mario, who helplessly flung up his hands as the bearers of his inevitable death reached him like tidal waves crashing on a seashore.

"Yeah!" Pedro exclaimed in sadistic delight as the car hit Mario Fernandez.

One moment the kid was staring at them in horror over the front of the Honda's hood, and the next moment both he and his wheelchair had vanished beneath the hood to the accompaniment of a horrible crunching and scraping noise.

"Damn, we missed his sister!" David groaned as he swerved the vehicle back onto the road again.

Pedro too had noticed. He was looking behind David; gazing through the rear window at Adriana, who was still lying in a heap, as if she'd stunned herself when she'd fallen.

"Quick, turn the car around let's run her over too!" Pedro yelled at David.

"I'm trying, I'm trying!" David called back, with mixed irritation and frustration in his voice. "I think the damn kid is stuck under the car."

Pedro looked behind them. There was no sign of the kid they'd just run over, just a short bloody trail dotted with bits of shattered metal and what might be mangled body tissue. At the same time, he and David Luiz now became aware of a very loud grating sound coming from beneath them, like they were dragging something along under them.

Realizing that what was causing both the sound and their bumpy ride were the remains of Mario and his wheeled metal conveyance filled Pedro with a sudden feeling of nausea. He'd killed people before, but never like this.

"Dammit, this kid's death is gonna make the news in a very big way," David said, while wrestling with the steering wheel. He was half speaking to himself as if he'd read Pedro's thoughts on the matter.

"Sick, dude, but we gotta get her too!" Pedro told David. "She's gotten up now, but she's still looking shell-shocked. Turn the car around before she realizes we're coming after her too and tries to run away!"

"Oh, she ain't going nowhere!" David said coldly, finally swerving the car around in a tight circle and barely missing hitting an oncoming taxi in the process.

After David got the car turned around, he felt a massive bump from the corpse they were dragging with them, but disregarded it. The vehicle was stolen anyway, they'd wipe it down for fingerprints and then discard it.

David saw what Pedro had been telling him about Adriana. Mario's older sister was standing on the sidewalk, staring at the bloody mess in the road with her mouth open. She looked unsure if she should scream, faint, or take off running down the street to save her own life. She looked over at their car as it neared her, and then, apparently unable to comprehend that it was about to kill her too, resumed staring at the road as if wondering what magic trick had made Mario vanish or transform into the red smear.

"This is too easy," David Luiz told Pedro. "We hit her and keep on rolling. The street is deserted again."

"Goodbye, puta!" Pedro yelled when the car was just ten yards from Adriana, who was still making no move to get out of their way. "Goodbye, snitch bit—"

But a loud bang under them announced that something had just gone wrong with their transport.

Ever since David had gotten the Accord turned around, a sharp fragment of the wheelchair had been forced against the car's right offside tire, slicing into its hardened rubber. Now, as David once more muscled the steering wheel to cut off any last-moment chance of Adriana escaping them, the metal spear finally punctured the tire.

Bang! The tire exploded. And just like that, David and Pedro's murderous plans were derailed. The corpse they were dragging along had already made the car almost impossible to maneuver and now that they'd also lost a tire, David lost control of the car completely.

After completely missing Adriana Fernandez by almost five yards, the white Honda Accord slewed back down off the pavement and back into the road, and then, seeming piloted by its morbid half-human/half-wheelchair rudder, skidded directly toward a large truck speeding in the opposite direction.

Just like had previously happened to Mario, now it was David and Pedro who flung up their hands as they realized that the crash was inevitable.

"Oh, God, no!" Pedro screamed at the two vehicles collided.

The result was a massive explosion as both vehicles caught on fire and burnt together. But even before this occurred, both David and Pedro had been crushed to death in the collision—because, ironically, they had stolen an old vehicle with a faulty airbag mechanism. All the explosion achieved was to incinerate their mangled corpses.

Across the road from the fiercely burning wreckage of the two crashed vehicles, Adriana had finally realized that the completely shapeless warped mess of flesh and metal lying in the road a short distance behind the burning white car was the remains of her younger brother Mario.

Her response in this situation was completely natural. She fainted.

CHAPTER 16

Shortly after David and Pedro began their murderous attempt to run down Adriana and Mario, another car with similar bad intent cruised another street five miles away. This car, a navy-blue Toyota, was also stolen and was being driven by a young black woman named Rosina. Rosina was David's new girlfriend and was also a member of *As Cobras Negras*.

Seated beside Rosina in the front of the car was Joao Ramires. Joao had a gun with him.

Concentrating their search on the red-light districts where the prostitutes frequented, the pair were cruising the streets of downtown Belém, looking for Tomás Barbosa, younger brother of the late Renato.

Tonight's plan was to dispose of all the incriminating evidence against Joao Ramires at the same time.

"I don't know where Tomás can be," Joao told Rosina, his voice dripping with a mixture of both fear and irritation. He was wearing his hoodie again, though after his last experience when he'd been arrested, he had more or less lost all faith in disguises, and so he'd left the hood of his hoodie down, trusting more now both to the reticence of the denizens of the red-light district to get involved with the police, and to his murderous reputation to protect his identity. In addition, wearing sunglasses at night to hide his eyes struck him as pointless, seeing as he needed to see clearly while shooting at their target.

"Normally, at this time he is here getting drunk, along with José Martins," Joao went on. "We need to kill him too tonight, Rosina. Otherwise, he will run and hide from us."

"Or he might get you first, Joao," Rosina said in her quiet voice. "I heard he has vowed to kill you if the judges don't jail you for life. They say it is only Tomás' desire to see you rot behind bars that has kept the other members of *Os Vermelhos* from coming after you themselves."

"That is just empty talk, Rosina," Joao snapped at her. "*Os Vermelhos* have all the courage of chickens. Where were they after we took out Carlito, huh? All they do is talk big, but they have no fighting spirit to back up their tough words."

Rosina shrugged and turned the car onto the next street. "I'm not debating it, Joao. All I'm saying is that if we miss Tomás tonight, you need to be extra-careful. *Os Vermelhos* may still be confused as to who killed Carlito and Maria, but you can be certain they will put two and two together once they hear that the two Fernandez siblings have also been killed tonight."

Joao nodded and grudgingly conceded her point. "You're right, Rosina." He pointed to an empty space between two cars parked at the roadside. "Park here. We'll wait a few minutes, then you can drive us back again."

Rosina parked and Joao pulled out his cellphone. He dialed, stared at the screen in some anger and then put the phone away again.

"You can't get David on the phone?" Rosina asked, with a little worry in her voice. "I hope nothing has gone wrong over there."

Joao shook his head and got out a pack of cigarettes. "Nothing can go wrong. Someone told me Adriana always goes to the market near her house at about this time on Sunday evenings."

"And her brother? What if she doesn't take him along on her shopping trip?"

Joao shrugged and offered Rosina a cigarette too. "I admit that that is the weakness of the plan," he said as she took a cigarette from the pack. He waited till he'd gotten out his lighter before going on: "But it's not a real problem. The kid is in a wheelchair, he can't run anywhere. If they miss him this evening, we'll have to visit their house in the midnight hours and get rid of him."

Joao lit both of their cigarettes.

"Doesn't all this killing bother you, Joao?" Rosina asked after taking a long pull on her cigarette. She turned on the radio and tapped the wheel along to some Brazilian hip-hop music.

Joao blew out smoke and then shook his head. "Maybe a week ago. But now, since that idiot judge says he's trying to get me the death penalty, it has become a case of kill-or-be-killed. Maybe I don't want to kill all of these people, but if I don't get rid of them all, I'll be killed instead." He stared coldly at Rosina through their shared curtains of cigarette smoke. "Do you get me?"

She nodded hastily back. "Oh, I get you, Joao. One can never be too careful when protecting one's own neck."

Joao nodded and relaxed. He'd had some reservations when Rosina had volunteered to drive the car, but they were gone now. During their planning for this hit, the gang *As Cobras Negras* had a choice of either Rosina or Mario Gomes for driver, but Mario was well known around here in the red-light districts. Seeing him might put out red flags for Tomás' friends; and they might then advise him not to show up tonight, or worse still, to plan an ambush for his would-be attackers.

Of course, the other problem when committing a crime with a woman as your partner was their tendency to get emotionally worked up over things. But, for the moment at least, the young black woman seated beside Joao was the picture of calm. Rosina had a gun too, in her handbag, but this was merely in case of emergencies. Joao was the triggerman.

They finished their cigarettes and then Joao said. "Okay, Rosina, let's start again. This time start with the street where old Gunther has his bar. I've heard talk of a girl there that Tomás likes."

"Okay, Joao." Rosina nodded and put the car in motion again.

This time they had more luck. Barely had they turned into the street than they saw Tomás walking along in the company of his friend José Martins Junior, the leader of *Os Vermelhos*, and a woman. Rosina slowed the car down to almost a crawling pace so they could observe the trio. Tomás and his companions seemed a little tipsy and were passing a bottle of liquor between them.

"Yes, now we have him," Joao said. He laughed meanly. "You too will die tonight, Tomás, and then I'll have nothing more to worry about in this stinking city."

However, there was a problem. Tomás, José, and their lady friend were approaching the car on the left side of the road, the driver's side, and from the opposite direction. This meant that Joao would have to lean over Rosina to fire at Tomás, which was too complicated and left room for errors.

"What do we do now?" he asked Rosina as they approached their quarry.

Rosina too, had quickly surmised the difficulty. "No problem, Joao, I'll drive past them and then turn the car around. "They've stopped by the lamp post now. I can get back here before they resume moving."

Joao nodded. Rosina was right. Tomás, José and the woman were laughing at something, with the woman pointing at a nearby barbeque stand while gripping her belly as if she was about to fall over.

Rosina already had the car moving. José peeked in the window as it rolled past them, winked at Rosina, and then turned back to his friends. He didn't notice Joao, who'd taken the precaution of quickly looking out of the passenger side window when he'd noticed José turning their way.

"Pretty lady," José remarked as the car left the trio behind.

As they reached the corner where Rosina would make the turn, Joao figured he could have shot and killed Tomás easily just now if he and José's lady friend hadn't been standing in the way.

Rosina got to the corner and made the turn.

"What are you waiting for?" Joao asked, when she stopped and waited for a black SUV carrying a load of girls to drive past them.

"The car gives us some cover, Joao," Rosina explained. "If we keep behind it, Tomás won't see us until it's too late."

Joao agreed that she was right. Everything would be over soon; all his worries flushed away like drowned rats going down a storm drain. His finger tightened over the grip of the gun in his lap.

The female behind the wheel of the black SUV was driving slowly, but not too slowly. Rosina too, had instinctively slowed down, leaving enough of a gap for her to pull their car out into the opposite lane to overtake the SUV once Joao had killed Tomás.

But then, right beside the streetlight where Tomás and his friends were laughing and drinking, the black SUV pulled up to an abrupt halt.

"Oh, God, what now?" Joao grumbled as a crowd of six half-naked young woman disembarked from the SUV at once.

"Their skimpy dressing means they're dancers," Rosina remarked. "They must be going to that club across the road. There's nowhere to park over on that side, so she's stopping here instead."

"No problem. We'll just wait for her to—"

But things weren't to be that simple. The arrival of so many barely-dressed young women had alerted the attention of the young men along the street, Tomás and José amongst them.

At first Tomás and José both turned to stare at the dancers, and began catcalling and flirting with them. But then, once the girls left the SUV and crossed the road towards their club destination, José Martins Junior happened to look past the vehicle they'd alighted from, to the Toyota idling behind it. At first his gaze fell on Rosina, whom he recognized from her previous drive past, and he smiled seductively at her.

However, he soon looked away from Rosina and noticed Joao in the passenger seat beside her. On seeing Joao, his eyes instantly widened in recognition, and he hurriedly turned back to Tomás. He began shaking Tomás and yelling at him.

"Dammit!" Joao growled in anger on realizing that the element of surprise had been lost. Gun held ready to fire, he quickly pushed the car door open and leapt out.

The partially drunken Tomás had turned to see what José was so alarmed about. He saw Joao at about the same time as Joao began firing at him.

By then, however, José was already pulling Tomás and the woman away from danger. And Joao was now also impaired by his own desire to not hit any of the bystanders near Tomás; the one thing he didn't need now were more dead people not connected with Renato's death.

So, Joao's first bullet hit the lamp post and ricocheted into the black SUV, shattering its rear window, and making the female chauffeur yelp in fright. Joao's second shot caught the panicking Tomás in the arm. But ironically, that shot also saved Tomás' life, as its impact spun him around and made it easier for his friends to pull him through the doorway of the nearest shop.

Joao took aim and fired once more at Tomás, but it was a wasted shot that only served to chip away a chunk of the wall. He angrily watched the shop door slam shut behind Tomás and the other two, and realized that now, while no one could possibly have recognized him, because everyone was panicking and taking cover from their expectation of additional gunfire, now was the best time to leave the crime scene.

Seething with frustration, he leapt back into the navy-blue Toyota.

"Go, girl, go!" he spat at Rosina, who immediately gunned the car into motion.

With a loud screech of tires, she swung the car out from behind the SUV and into the scant flow of oncoming traffic, made a few daredevil turns, and barely half a minute later, had them safely four streets away.

"Did you get Tomás?" she asked, her dark face beaming with excitement. "Is he dead now?"

"I only scared the life out of him," Joao said in disgust. "But no, the son-of-a-bitch isn't dead."

They got out of their stolen car, wiped it clean of fingerprints and abandoned it for the police to find.

CHAPTER 17

For the entire week after Mario's death, Adriana survived each day by the sheer force of the human organism's ingrained habit of living—meaning that, she went on living simply because she didn't know how to die.

What had happened seemed impossible to her. The scene endlessly replayed through her mind: the old white car veering off the street and coming towards she and Mario . . . she doing her best to roll his wheelchair to safety and then when the wheelchair defiantly seemed rooted to the spot, trying to muscle Mario out of it and fling him to safety . . . how much dead weight he'd been . . . how scared he'd been . . . then at very last minute flinging herself to safety . . . stunned, but hearing Mario scream, along with a terrifying screech of shredding metal . . . getting to her feet again and seeing that same car, skewing about wildly like its driver couldn't control it, with a messy red trail behind it. . . and then, the same white car making a line for her also, only this time she wasn't really aware of its presence; she'd been too confused as to where her brother had suddenly vanished to . . . the car missing her, swerving wildly across the road . . . the explosion, the fire . . . the thing in the road that looked like it had once been human, but couldn't be, because humans had heads and limbs, and this bleeding unrecognizable thing only had bloody ribs and wheels . . . blessed darkness as the realization of what she was staring at finally hit her . . .

For a fortnight, Adriana replayed everything through her mind endlessly, like the crazy images of Mario's death were a record stuck in a loop. The images were there in the morning when she woke up; they haunted her throughout her waking hours and also formed her nightmares when she slept, if she slept at all.

***

The police had no clues as to who had done it. Even though they thought it might be murder, lack of evidence forced them to treat the case as an accident.

Adriana had told them everything that had happened, and they were extremely sympathetic, especially due to the fresh public outrage that Mario's death had provoked in the media. The public was especially irate that the boy had died just before realizing his dream of entering medical school.

Yes, it really did seem as if the deadly vehicle and its occupants had deliberately targeted Adriana and her younger brother, the investigating detectives (once more Wagner and Lopes) both agreed, but this suspicion had to be tempered by Adriana's own statement that the vehicle had appeared out of control at the time, in addition to which the forensics people had found several scorched beer cans in the charred husk that had remained of the burnt car. So, the two men had definitely been drinking, which of course threw the original theory of murderous intent into doubt.

Also, it was equally possible that after hitting Mario, the driver had tried to turn the car around to see if Adriana was okay and had once again lost control of his vehicle.

There were additional problems. Yes, the vehicle had been stolen, but all that remained of the two thieves were charred chunks of bone and ash piles that defied investigation. Other than deducing that they had been male, the police had no way to identify who the two occupants of the deadly car had been.

Yes, the Belém police had initially had their suspicions that Joao Ramires might be involved, but when the deaths had occurred, Joao had been seen in a bar drinking with a young black woman. So even if he was someway implicated in Mario's death, there was currently no evidence to break his alibi.

In her dazed state, Adriana heard all of this with resignation.

Mario was gone . . . gone, gone, gone, snatched away from this life as if by a tornado.

As was natural in such matters, however, the public soon lost interest in the case, particularly since no new developments came to light. One or two journalists tried to link the 'attack' on Adriana and Mario to a supposed gangland shooting that same night, in which Tomás Barbosa, another witness in the case against Joao Ramires, had been wounded, but they found no witnesses who had seen the shooter. Even Tomás' friend José Martins Junior, who had been the one to first notice the assassin getting out of his car, said he'd not seen the shooter's face. As for Tomás Barbosa? He had dropped out of sight since the shooting, and the investigating journalists had found it impossible to reach him for comment.

And then there was a huge political scandal about a politician sleeping with his stepdaughter and everyone seemingly forgot about Mario Fernandez altogether.

***

Mario's funeral came and went, with both Adriana and her mother Bruna leaning on each other for support.

Adriana had no idea which of them was the worst hit by Mario's death. At times it seemed to her that her mother was coping with their loss better than she was, but then she realized what was really going on; after the previous devastating experience of the death of her husband, Bruna Fernandez had simply become a lot better at internalizing her grief. Occasionally, Adriana saw her mother sitting by a window, staring out emptily into the distance. At any other time, Adriana would have been very concerned about her mother's delicate frame of mind, but right now, she felt exactly the same way.

The one thing that helped her cope with her pain was her music. And so, for a few hours each day, she locked herself in her room and played her instrument and sang to herself to assuage her trauma.

***

But despite the solace Adriana found in playing her music, leaving Sistema de Música had now become a no-brainer. All of the band members, including Vanessa, had been immensely supportive of her throughout this trying period, and yet she now felt deep inside herself that it was time for her to move on.

The band hadn't had a rehearsal since Carlito's death, and Adriana's state of mind following Mario's death had meant she'd been unable to perform with them at the Paradise Club, the keyboard playing for those gigs had been handled by Daniel's younger brother, Marcelo.

But one evening, Gabriel came over to her house and they sat in the living room together to discuss what Adriana wanted to do as far as the band was concerned. She was grateful to him for not bringing Vanessa along.

"I need a break from the band," she told him. "Too much has happened too fast, starting with the club shooting. I just want to forget everything for a while. I need time to myself, time to clear my mind."

"Yeah," Gabriel quickly agreed. "Maybe, you taking a break from Sistema de Música would be all for the best, Addy."

Adriana was surprised; Gabriel actually looked relieved at the news that she would no longer be playing with them. But then, she thought she understood why this was: her leaving the band would mean there would be no chance of she and Vanessa coming into conflict over him.

***

One night, several days after Mario's death, Bruna Fernandez summoned her grieving daughter into her bedroom.

"Listen to me, child," she said, once Adriana was seated beside her on her bed, "I'm not fooled by anything, and neither should you be. We both know that, no matter what the police say, it was Joao who had your brother killed."

Adriana nodded as she regarded her mother's age-and-worry-creased face. She too had been thinking the same; but it was a worry she would rather not dwell on, or else she knew she would become paranoid.

"I'm very certain that Joao won't stop until he kills you too," Bruna went on, now taking Adriana's hands in her own and squeezing them. "You need to leave Belém for a while. Joao's trial is still several months off. Much can go wrong for you in that time if you remain here." She sighed. "Daughter of mine, I'm already bereaved of my husband and my son—two times for my son—I don't want to attend your own funeral as well."

"Are you saying I shouldn't testify against Joao?" Adriana asked her mother.

Bruna shook her head. "No, I'm not saying that. The police would never accept your change of statement, anyhow. But you need to leave Belém, until it is time for the trial to commence." Her mother nodded at her own words and then added: "Maybe go and stay with my sister Julia."

"That's too far away, mama," Adriana protested on hearing this. Acará, where Aunt Julia lived, was almost eighty kilometers, or fifty miles, away.

"The farther you are from Joao, the better for you, and for my nerves also. Or what is to stop him or his associates from climbing into our windows one night and slitting your throat? Child, you might think the public are rooting for you to put him behind bars. Yes, maybe they are, but didn't they root for your brother also? And since he died, did anyone we didn't already know bring even a rose to pay his respects to us? Have the police or the prosecutors assigned us a guard to keep us safe? No, they haven't, Adriana. So, no, at the moment, daughter, it isn't justice that counts, but survival."

***

Adriana took her mother's advice to heart and began thinking of how to get away from Belém. However, she still felt Acará was far, but maybe not fare enough to flee to.

In addition, even at the best of times, Acará was a very boring place to live in. As far as she could tell, Acará hardly had a music scene worth thinking about, and threats to her life notwithstanding, she didn't intend to stagnate musically, particularly since her music was the main thing helping her cope with this latest tragedy in her life.

In the meantime, however, before she made up her mind on what exactly to do, Adriana took the precaution of leaving home and moving in with a girlfriend of hers.

CHAPTER 18

"I went to the puta's house to slit her throat, but she wasn't there!" Mario Gomes angrily told Joao and Rosina a few days later, as the three of them huddled around cold beers in a local bar near David's apartment. Mario Gomes was a short, fat, bearded man with very cold eyes. "I asked around the neighbors and they're all claiming she has fled the country for fear of you, Joao."

"That can't be true," Joao retorted. "I'm sure the police have hidden her away until the trial." They were keeping their voices lowered, but the bar was mostly empty anyway.

Rosina spat angrily on the floor. "Missing Tomás that night was bad luck," she said. "Now he is missing too." Rosina was still very upset at David's death.

"Forget about Tomás," Mario Gomes coldly told Rosina. "The kid has no guts at all. Once Joao put that bullet in him, he panicked and ran for the south border. Last thing I hear about him, he was in Chile."

The three of them had a good laugh about that. Joao ordered a fresh round of beers and two plates of roasted pork.

"Well, what matters is that Tomás is now out of the witness picture," Mario said. "We can be certain he won't be back to testify against Joao. So now, the only witness we need worry about is the Fernandez woman, Adriana."

"Maybe it is true that she has left Brazil," Rosina angrily stated. "Ah, but that is so sad. Me, I hold her personally responsible for David's death. I want to kill her myself. Even more now than Joao does."

"So long as she dies, I'm fine with you killing her, Rosina," Joao said grimly. "But the problem is, if the police are hiding her, there is no way for us to reach her. Then, once the trial comes, they produce her like a magic trick and I'm for the noose."

"There are many ways to skin a cat," Mario Gomes said, after lighting a cigarette and taking a pull on it. "If both Tomás and Adriana can hide, then so too can you, Joao."

"Huh?" Joao stared at Mario. Up to this point, the idea of hiding hadn't suggested itself to him. "What do you mean, hide?"

Mario Gomes laughed coldly. "I spoke to our lawyer, and he tells me that our case now is a very weak one, and it would be a lot better if you weren't around to answer it. He said, seeing as you're on trial for murder, jumping bail is a minor addition to your crimes. And besides, my friend, if it saves your neck from the hangman's rope, why not?"

Joao nodded. He understood what his friend meant. The gang's original plan, once all the witnesses had been disposed of, was to have David and Pedro insist that Joao had shot Renato Barbosa in self-defense after Renato lunged at him with a knife. David and Pedro had already stated as much to the police on the night of the murder. But now that both David and Pedro were dead—Joao hated to think that they had been roasted up like chunks of beef—now they were dead, neither man could testify in court. And so, when the police produced Adriana from where they were currently keeping her safe, and if just possibly, Tomás did garner up sufficient courage to return to Belém and testify at his brother's trial, Joao's goose would truly be cooked.

"Okay, so I need to hide," Joao agreed.

"But where can you go?" Rosina asked. "The Brazilian police won't let you out of the country."

"Leave that to me," Mario Gomes said. "I've already thought this through before bringing it up."

"What do you have in mind?" Joao asked Mario.

They paused their conversation for a while, while the bartender set down their fresh beers and a tray of food. When he left, Mario Gomes replied to Joao's question:

"Joao, are you still in touch with that gringa you said you dated when you visited your brother in America? The nightclub waitress." Mario took a drag on his cigarette. "Where does she live again?"

"Oh, Corrine?" Joao nodded. "Yeah, we're still in touch on Facebook. She keeps asking when I'll be visiting again. She lives in Cleveland, in the state of Ohio."

"Good," Mario said, puffing out cigarette smoke, then pointing the cigarette at Joao to make his point. "Get in touch with her. Tell her you'll be visiting in two weeks' time and ask if she can put you up."

"Why not just ask Ricardo?"

"Because, your brother's place is the first place the authorities will check once they're unable to find you here."

"Okay, I'll do it," Joao agreed. "But, in just two weeks? My passport is long expired. Getting a fake one may take me up to a month."

"Yeah," Rosina asked, taking Mario's cigarette from his fingers. "How is he gonna leave the country and get to the USA with everyone looking for him?"

Mario Gomes laughed. "That part is easy. He will travel using Pedro's passport."

Rosina and Joao both looked at Mario as if he was crazy. "Are you nuts?" Rosina asked.

Mario shook his head. "No, I'm not. You both know that Pedro shared an apartment with me. I know where his passport is and I've checked that it's still valid; best of all, Pedro has a valid multiple-entry visa to the USA that doesn't expire till next year June." Mario sipped some of his new beer and forked up a chunk of roast pig. "But, most important for us, Pedro also looked almost like Joao, just that he was a little thinner. But once Joao grows a mustache and cuts his hair, they could be the same person."

Mario burst out laughing again, then continued: "And best of all, there's no way for the customs authorities to tell the difference between both of them, because they've not yet registered Pedro as being dead, since his body was too badly burnt up in the car crash for the police to positively identify him. As such, no one knows Pedro is dead yet, so we can use his still valid ID to smuggle our man Joao here out of the country."

Rosina nodded. "Yeah, man, I like Mario's plan. And then, Joao, whenever Adriana resurfaces from wherever the police are hiding her, we'll kill her and then give you the all-clear to return home a free man."

"Oh," Joao said with a broad grin. "This sounds like it'll work."

***

And so, that was exactly what they did. Two weeks from that day, Joao Ramires, now sporting a mustache and with his hair cut short, boarded an aircraft out of Brazil en-route for the United States of America.

In the meantime, his ex-girlfriend Corrine Phillips (who was currently between lovers) had happily assured him that once he was in the USA, he could stay with her for as long as he wanted.

CHAPTER 19

Adriana of course, had no idea that her erstwhile pursuer had left Brazil. To her mind the threat of Joao Ramires suddenly attacking her was a clear and present danger. He was out of sight but not at all out of her mind.

Sometimes she even dreamt of him killing her.

It was while Adriana was still trying to make up her mind where to hide for the moment, that the pandemic, that most unwelcome of modern travelers, arrived in Brazil.

One of the first effects of the global pandemic was that unnecessary travel across the country was curtailed, meaning that now Adriana couldn't leave Belém even if she wanted to.

Another effect was that all trials were postponed to uncertain future dates, so that there was now no telling when Joao would be appearing in court.

The months passed with the pandemic taking away many in its jaws of death. Adriana and their mother both survived. Whenever Adriana saw her mother saying a Rosary and weeping silent tears as she remembered her dead husband and son, she wondered if their survival in the face of worldwide death was because God Almighty still had more suffering in store for their already devastated family.

Throughout this dark period, Adriana had had no news of Joao. No one that she knew had seen him either. There were different rumors about him. Some people claimed he'd died in the pandemic, some said he'd committed an offence in another Brazilian state and had been arrested by the police there. The latest rumor Adriana had heard placed Joao outside of the country, either in Mexico or in the USA, where his younger brother Ricardo lived.

Personally, she hoped he'd died in the pandemic. *Then I would be free of him for good, and not have to worry any longer!*

Adriana still often felt intense grief. And during this time, when she felt as if her world was falling apart, she developed the habit of visiting the seaside. She had nothing to do there, but she found it oddly comforting to sit on the rocky Belém beach, staring out across the ocean, to God-knows-where.

The gulls in the sky, the distant waves, the endless blue, were all mirrors of something in her mind that she found hard to express in words, or even sometimes in her thoughts; but occasionally she was able to put a word to it—escape. Yes, the endless expanse of water facing her as she traced her way along the seashore, reflected her desire to escape her current situation. Not just now for her own safety, but also simply to get out of this miserable life she had so far lived.

But for the moment, escape seemed impossible. Even if Bruna claimed otherwise, Adriana knew that her mother needed her. So, she remained at home and continued the daily struggle for survival.

But then one day, seemingly out of the blue, things changed for Adriana. Out that day at a supermarket buying groceries, she ran into a musician friend who told her about the FiestaAqua cruise line, who were currently hiring musicians for their cruise ships.

"Me and the guys auditioned," Rodrigo informed her in drawled Portuguese that suggested he was a little high. "But they're full up with bands. Not so with lounge acts tho'—they're still looking for those. You should definitely give it a shot."

He gave Adriana the details for the audition, and they parted ways.

Once she was back home from shopping, Adriana called up for an audition for the sea cruise. The next day, she was quickly accepted; the fact that she could speak English helping her chances, as their newest ship, the CasaAqua, was scheduled for a Caribbean and Bahamian rotation of voyages over the next nine months—meaning a major percentage of its passengers would be English speakers.

Her mother Bruna was delighted to see her leave. "Go with God, daughter, and remain safe," she said during their parting at the Belém docks.

Adriana kissed her mother on both cheeks, climbed the gangplank, waved goodbye and departed into her new life.

CHAPTER 20

Adriana stared out at the endless expanse of ocean, much like she had back home in Brazil, with the difference that here there was no land anywhere in sight. The ocean liner rocked with the movement of the sea and she smiled. She was used to the ship's constant movement now, but at first it had been a difficult transition to make from solid ground; the seasickness pills had only helped a little.

The ship rocked again. The air had a dampness to it that suggested rain.

They were floating out somewhere in the mid-Atlantic. Adriana thought they were currently off the coast of Panama, en-route to the USA. It was early evening; she was on a break between lounge shifts. She often spent this time of day like this, up on the aft deck, leaning over the railing and staring into the distance.

I can't really complain, she thought. *This job pays really well. And best of all, Mama sounds happy each time I talk to her, like she's no longer totally depressed over Mario's death.*

At the moment, Adriana was sending almost all her salary home to her mother. Living on the ship, she didn't require much for her personal maintenance.

As much as possible, she tried not to think about Mario, because thoughts of him filled her with depression. Instead of the sadness, she had the happiness of her music. She immersed herself in her job on the cruise and to her relief, discovered that focusing on the music was enough both to occupy her and sooth her otherwise troubled soul.

Unusual for this time of day, she was alone up here on the tenth deck. Her sole companion on the back side of the ship at the moment was a seagull that had landed to take a rest from its constant circling overhead. The bird was at the far end of the deck, perched on the wooden rail and staring out over the sea—just like she was. Her gaze swept out across the water again, and then she got out her cellphone from her pocket. She was able to get the internet from the ship's satellite hook-up. Although frequently patchy, it worked today. She checked her emails, checked Facebook, and realized it would soon be time for her first performance.

Adriana mostly played samba tunes and jazz standards; stuff like *Oye Como Va* and *The Girl from Ipanema*, and *Let it Be* or *In The Mood*; songs everyone was familiar with. She'd found Elton John songs to be a particular hit with the Americans. Sometimes she played classical piano pieces—simple adaptations of familiar orchestral pieces. She sang too when the mood took her, a mixture of both old and new songs, with several of her own compositions thrown in.

There were six musical acts on the CasaAqua cruise, one for each musical lounge. There were also two DJs and a Karaoke bar. The acts rotated between the lounges on a fixed timetable, and so the passengers knew that if they wanted to dance on Wednesday night, all they had to do was head down to the *Electric Lounge* on Deck Eight where Soul Bob & The Popcorn Club would be laying out a solid disco beat for one and all. Or if they were younger travelers, they could check out DJ Vibesoul in the *Silhouette Club* for EDM. Tonight, Adriana was in *Embers*, a mahogany decorated classy club on Deck Seven, and expected to be serenading primarily older folk. *Embers* also served as a cigar lounge during different nights and Adriana was glad that this evening wasn't one of those times.

Sometimes she sat in with one of the bands. That was fun—it allowed her to mingle and helped keep loneliness at bay.

She'd been working on the CasaAqua cruise ship for nearly six months. During that period, she hadn't been home once. Although she frequently thought of her mother, she still didn't feel compelled to return to Belém anytime soon. *Too many memories, too much danger.* The bubble of safety provided by the cruise ship itself sailing its routes to the various ports of call seemed to calm her—at least for now. Still. . .

Maybe it would be better if I had a boyfriend. But try as I might, there's no one here that even catches my fancy; no one I've so far met that I feel any real connection with.

This however, was really only part of the problem. Additionally, she felt reluctant, not to mention nervous, about starting a relationship with anyone. Each time she saw a man she liked even a little bit, the memory of what had transpired between Gabriel, Vanessa and herself came to the forefront of her mind and she felt repulsed by what had happened. She found it hard to put the blame on either Gabriel or Vanessa; she believed she had only herself to blame for losing out back then.

I'd known Gabriel for three years and nothing happened between us. And then Vanessa comes along, and in less than a month . . .

Adriana was relieved that she'd come out of it with her head held high. Of course a major part of her coping with what had happened was due to Mario's tragic death. Once that had happened—just two days after she'd discovered that Gabriel and Vanessa were now lovers—nothing else had mattered; definitely not something as relatively minor as a heartbreak. But still, Adriana occasionally thought about the past, and her recollections stood before her like a wall that blocked off fresh romantic inclination.

She grew tired of standing by the railing and stepped away from it to sit in a deck chair. She looked down the deck. Her companion the seagull had just taken to the air again, startled away by the emergence of a family of four from the ship's interior.

Adriana Fernandez lay back in the deckchair; shut her eyes and tried to relax.

PART TWO:
TOM & MAGGIE

CHAPTER 21

The Jazzy Truth jazz club was situated in the middle of Main Street, in the town of Wheeling, West Virginia. Jazzy Truth was a small and comfortable venue, begun in the late 80's by a grocer and jazz enthusiast named Clive Bronson. Clive played the saxophone, and he began the club as a place where he could jam with his musical friends. He'd initially run it only on the weekends, but then a sequence of unexpected circumstances had brought the club to regional notice, and a number of popular jazzers had begun stopping by the venue on their way east or west, and suddenly Clive had found himself with a prospering musical business on his hands.

Fast-forward forty years, and today the Jazzy Truth was run by Clive's daughter Maggie. Maggie Duchensky was forty-three years old; an attractive, compact brunette with a slight predisposition to worry about things.

At the moment, while trying not to worry about it, Maggie Duchensky was currently wishing that the prosperous musical period she remembered from her childhood would return. For her club, that was. Other musical genres seemed to be doing just great; kids were making records and videos and doing tours all over the world. But jazz seemed to have been left behind.

Wheeling was always known as a small Nashville with country music dominating the scene. This was mostly due to Jamboree USA, a live country-western show performed on a weekly basis from the Capitol Theatre, just a few blocks away. This show was broadcast all over the country on radio and now over the Internet. Opened in 1928, the Capitol Theatre, and its weekly country broadcasts were still going strong.

At least it seemed that way to Maggie, who tried to remember the last time her little musical venue had had a full house.

Maybe I should just pack it in, she thought. *Sell the property like Tom says and invest the proceeds in something else.*

But deep down, she knew she wouldn't do that. Too much of her personal history was invested in this place. She'd grown up around music and could vividly recall the aged black trumpet virtuoso Fats Walker, tousling her hair when she was barely five years old and grinning down at her. All the old jazz greats had been friends of her father; and their love and passion for music had transferred itself to her. Oddly enough, Maggie wasn't musical herself, but the jazzmen's pleasure and love of their art now flourished in her.

So now, Maggie was hooked on the music too. It was rooted deep in her, and a feeling like that meant one couldn't simply pack up and leave when the going got tough; one had to stay and roll with the punches.

But for the past half-year it had been hard going; the punches had kept on coming and Maggie was growing punch-drunk from rolling with them.

The problem wasn't the club patrons. Even aside from its reputation as a jazz haunt, the Jazzy Truth had a regular drinking clientele, local folks who gathered either to have a good time or to drown their sorrows in their beers. But these drinkers barely paid the bills and the bartender's salary.

A lot more is needed to get this place back on its feet again, Maggie acknowledged as she crossed to the bar and told the bartender Eddie to pour her a drink. It was early evening and she figured it wasn't too early for some alcohol.

"Here you go," Eddie said, sliding a glass of wine over to her. Eddie was a tall young man who doubled as the building's janitor and lived in one of the two apartments over the club. Maggie and her husband Tom lived about a mile down the road in their own house. It was good having Eddie living on the property in case of break-ins. There wasn't much that cost much in the building; but most of what was in the club held great sentimental value for Maggie.

"You're thinking 'bout how to get the musician's back here, aren't ya?" Eddie asked Maggie when she lowered her glass.

"You read my mind," she replied glumly. "Eddie, what the hell are we gonna do? It's like the pandemic flushed the jazz toilet, so to speak."

Eddie played jazz drums. Back when the club was flourishing he'd occasionally sat in with the itinerant musos. "Yeah, I know," he agreed, scratching his chin. "All that time spent sitting at home might have worked wonders for the kids with all their computers and programmed beats and stuff, but jazz has gotta be played live to live . . ." He sighed deeply. "And at the moment . . ."

". . . Yeah, I know. Jazz might as well be renamed 'dodo' for all the life it has left," Maggie finished for him, gesturing over to the raised performance stage in the far corner, where resided a lonely upright piano and a battered Fender Rhodes electric piano. "At least, here in Wheeling it is."

She finished her wine. Eddie picked up the bottle to pour her another glass, but she shook her head at him. "No, I'm driving and besides, it really is too early in the day to be drinking. If I get home smelling of booze, Tom is going to think I'm losing it."

Eddie nodded understandingly. "Don't worry. It's just a matter of time before the musicians remember this place and return."

"But when, Eddie? It's been six months since we last had a full house." She gestured around the empty bar and out through the door at the equally empty parking lot. "We're not exactly losing money, but we definitely aren't making any either." She scowled at the young bartender. "The only reason I can keep you on is because you agreed to work for less money."

He paused in polishing a glass and smiled. "I'm fine—I believe in this place. And besides, you're forgetting you're accommodating me too. No way is a young dude gonna turn down a cushy pad like I got over a few less dollars."

She laughed. "Ah, if only Jerry hadn't left when he did. I can time the downturn exactly to when he left for New York."

"It was a big gig, and afterwards they made a record. Eddie picked up his phone. "You seen 'em on YouTube?"

Maggie shook her head. "I didn't even know they'd made a record." Jerry Bennet had been the bar's resident pianist. Jerry was a virtuoso; it had only been a matter of time before a record label noticed his YouTube videos and promos and invited him out to do some session work for them.

Maggie wasn't bitter at Jerry for leaving when he did; she was just miffed that it had come when it did; when things were on a general downer.

Jerry had been a definite crowd-puller here at the club. Musicians and singers from neighboring towns had driven over to jam with him, even from as far away as Toledo, Ohio and as his reputation spread, so had the club's reputation. It had been a win-win situation for them both.

Eddie was showing her a YouTube video of Jerry's new band. She noted the page details. "Send me the page link—I'll watch it later. Damn, I wish I could find another virtuoso to take Jerry's place."

"Don't wanna discourage ya, but don't even look. Even an elephant can't fill shoes that big."

Maggie nodded. "That's what worries me," she said. "That's exactly what worries me."

CHAPTER 22

By dinner, Maggie's unease still hadn't subsided.

"What the matter with you, hon?" her husband Tom asked her as she fidgeted over her plate like an eagle unable to decide what to pounce on. "You've looked upset since I got home."

Tom Duchensky was a tall and fleshy man, one who dwarfed his petite wife. Forty-six-years-old come August, his black hair was rapidly thinning now at the front. His blue eyes however were as alive as ever, and even held some amusement as he regarded Maggie.

Maggie fidgeted with her steak some more and then put down her fork and knife. "It's the club, Tom. I can't stop wondering how to get the musicians back here."

Tom nodded while chewing a mouthful of steak. Then he said, "You just gotta hang in there, hon. It's a manifestation of the changing times. As far as I can tell, jazz is on its way out . . . yet again."

Maggie smiled at that. "Jazz is supposedly always on its way out. It's the dinosaur that refused to become extinct. Sometimes I wish it really would subside quietly into its grave of primordial musical ooze. Then I wouldn't care so much about it. I'd just move on to hosting gigs for the emo and grunge kids."

Tom nodded again around a fresh mouthful. "Yeah, every few years there's a jazz revival based around a new group of youngsters, and then the scene fizzles out again for another few years." He waved his fork at Maggie. "Hey, honey, I thought you were trying to get another pianist for the residency?"

She sighed. "I'm doing my best. But so far, no dice. I've found a few good guys, but no one even close to Jerry's class."

"Maybe you need to lower your standards. I've seen some reviews of Jerry's album. The critics are calling the kid 'a once-in-a-lifetime' talent."

Maggie sighed while chewing. "I know. Eddie was just telling me about it. I dunno, maybe you're right; maybe the best thing to do is hire one of the guys I've seen on YouTube—there's a passably good keyboard player who lives down the road in Pittsburgh he can form a trio with Eddie and Eddie's friend Eric . . ."

"That kid who plays the saxophone?" I thought you said he was too rough around the edges."

"He still is, but he lives nearby too. I'll just restrict them to playing well-known standards, nothing too demanding." She frowned. "Dammit, honey, I really wish we had some money to hire some out-of-town acts, even if it's just one weekend a month."

Tom grimaced. They had been over this before. Because their small city of Wheeling wasn't one of the main jazz meccas, for a little club like the Jazzy Truth there were really only two alternatives to attract elite jazz musicians. One was simply to offer them a lot of money to play the venue, so they could squeeze it in while doing a state tour of better-know jazz clubs, and the other was to strive to become unique in some way, so that musicians passing through the area added you to their itinerary because the venue had become a landmark, a place where other musicians met and exchanged ideas and riffs.

In the past the Jazzy Truth had benefited from taking the latter route. Musicians from all over the state and from out of state stopped by simply because they knew so-and-so was in the area and would also be stopping by for an impromptu jam session with whoever else was there at the time. It hadn't hurt in the least either that the club had decent audio recording facilities, so that each night's playing had been captured for posterity in digital high-fidelity.

That had all been very well and good; back then the club had made a consistent and large profit. However, what Maggie was currently suggesting/wishing to Tom wasn't well and good at all, and it showed on his face

Since the Jazzy Truth's downturn in fortunes, Tom had had to take on more and more work to keep he and Maggie's heads above water. He didn't get it: sometimes the movement of funds in and out of his bank account seemed like a sequence of magic tricks, almost like life was scamming him in some inexplicable way. Ten years ago, he and Maggie never expected to have so many bills to pay in their forties. But they did. Property mortgages, health and life insurance, taxes, and let's not forget the 401K payments so they wouldn't be stuck with living in a trailer after slaving all their lives . . . the list went on.

And they didn't even have kids. Tom wondered how their friends with kids coped.

He and Maggie weren't extravagant or anything like that, but the IT industry wasn't doing as well as it should be, and a software engineer like Tom could easily be considered surplus to requirements if he didn't put in more than his fair share of overtime. So, Tom was doing as much overtime as he could and also taking on several freelance software coding jobs as well. He frowned again. As far as he could tell, his current constant state of stress was starting to tell on his health, especially with the growing frequency of headaches he had been experiencing.

He paused eating for a moment, swiped on the screen of his cellphone and frowned.

Maggie noticed the look of displeasure on his face. "Oh, darling, don't look at me like that. You know I'm only *wishing* we had the money to bring in some outside talent. I know how hard you're working—I'm not about to pressure you or do anything unreasonable that will put an additional strain on our finances."

Tom shook his head at her. "It's not that, hon. He pointed to his cellphone. "I'm getting eyestrain from staring too long at computer and phone screens."

She looked concerned but waved it off. "Maybe you just need stronger reading glasses. You're not wearing them now, you know."

He shook his head again. "No, I don't think it's that. I think it's a sign of overwork. It's been happening in the office a lot lately.

Sometimes when I'm staring at the screen of my laptop, for a moment, everything seems to go blank. Then my eyes focus again, and everything is normal. Sometimes when it happens, I get a splitting headache, but it quickly passes."

Maggie looked worried. "What do you think is the matter?"

He shrugged back at her. "Like I just said, hon. Overwork. I've been spending too much time with those darn computers. If I'm not careful one of these days I'll wake up and begin hearing keyboard clacking noises in my head, you know, like the sound of those 8-bit video games."

Tom finished his reply with a laugh, and so Maggie laughed too, but it was clear from his face that he was concerned.

And exhausted too, Maggie thought. *OMG, how didn't I notice how worn-out Tom is? With the club not making any money, the worst thing that could possibly happen to us both now, would be for Tom to suffer either a nervous or a physical breakdown.*

"Listen, darling, you need a vacation," she said. "You've bound to have plenty of leave built up. How soon can you take it?"

He smiled. "Next week." Then he sighed. "But unless I'm well out of the country during my vacation, Delaney is certain to find something that needs handling in the office that I alone, with my superior IT kung-fu powers can tackle. And of course, he'll offer me a wonderful overtime bonus to temporarily return to work—a bonus I'll be unable to refuse because *we need* the money. So in essence, I'm totally unreachable, my next vacation will see me working as hard as ever."

Maggie nodded sagely. "Then, darling, we just need to ensure that you are out of the country during your next vacation."

Tom smiled. "I really wish it was that simple. I really wish we had the financial security to tell those guys to shove it and—"

"Oh, but it is that simple, darling," Maggie replied sweetly. "How would you like to go on a cruise?"

Tom first looked taken aback and then he laughed. "Oh, don't be silly, darling. We can't afford one of those."

She laughed at his surprise. "We can now."

"How?"

"Hold on a minute." She got to her feet and left the living room, returning a few seconds later with a large brochure. "Junk mail," she explained, walking around the table to stand beside him and then dropping the brochure on the dining table. "But, in this case, it's perfect for us, because the FiestaAqua cruise line are offering Caribbean cruises at heavily discounted rates."

Realizing she'd gotten his interest, Maggie opened up the brochure and together, they began to study the cabin rates for the CasaAqua cruise.

CHAPTER 23

Maggie, whose only previous travels from her hometown had been to the nearby states of Pennsylvania, Ohio and Indiana, loved the CasaAqua cruise ship. Once they'd set sail from Miami she was up and down its decks, looking into everything, while Tom sat on deck and tried not to throw up.

The ship was very large. Since childhood, Maggie had seen cruise ships in magazines and movies, but she couldn't get over how large they were in reality. This one they were on seemed about the size of a city block. Above the water it was twelve decks high, and as long as two football fields—she had no words!

The ship was so beautiful—and SO elegant! Plus, the staff really pampered them, greeting them on a first name basis and sharing with them excellent tips on how to have a truly fantastic time onboard.

She felt as if she and Tom were on a floating city-island in the middle of the ocean, the dark blue sea all around and without a care in the world.

She loved the feeling of disconnection from the insanity back home, from the rat race and violence.

Today was the fourth day that they'd been floating at ease over the blue. A day earlier, they visited Fiesta Cay, the cruise line's own private island in the Bahamas. Now, the CasaAqua was sailing towards Mexico.

"Wow! Why didn't we ever try this before?" she asked Tom as they relaxed on a posh sofa in the ship's middle deck. There were several other couples up here relaxing also. "As far as I can tell, the ship is only half-full." She took a sip of her coke. "You know, darling, we're getting service like this because the luxury liner industry almost died during the pandemic."

"As far as I'm concerned, the luxury liner industry can keep their discounts and great service," Tom groaned. "They can keep the sea too; do whatever they want with it. I haven't felt this unhappy since I was bullied in junior high."

Maggie giggled. "Oh, you should get over the seasickness by tomorrow, or I can pick you up some Dramamine from the ship's concession store now if you'd like?"

He scowled at her. "Life is so damn unfair sometimes. How come it's not bothering you like it is me?"

They were sitting side by side and she leaned over and kissed him. "Don't be jealous, darling, we can't all be perfect."

He grunted and resumed suffering in silence.

Maggie relaxed back in her seat. She wasn't bothered by Tom's behavior. Despite the nausea he was feeling from the ship's motion, he'd made it clear to her that he was delighted she'd persuaded him to take this trip with her. Already she could see it in both his eyes and his posture, that lessening of society's burdens that automatically occurred when society was too far away to be counted as relevant.

During lunch she had heard one of the ship's stewards tell a woman they'd shortly be docking in Costa Maya in the wee hours of the following morning.

As they leisurely sailed through the Gulf of Mexico, Tom finally felt that he was now far enough away from West Virginia to count as being "near home," as Tom's boss Delaney had realized yesterday, when, as predicted, he'd called Tom, asking if he could quickly drop by the office to have a look at something one of the interns had completely screwed up.

Delaney was fortunate to have caught Tom on the private island, else he wouldn't have reached his cell at all.

"Sorry, dude, but I ain't home right now. All I have in sight at the moment is water, sand, and a watermelon colada that is melting right now in my other hand. It's beautiful here. I'm drowning in the sky. Great view. I could do without the seasickness tho'."

A short period of explanation of exactly where he and Maggie were at that moment had resulted in Delaney's enquiring if Tom could work from home.

"I left the laptop back at the house. I didn't think I'd need it out here."

"You could have taken it with you."

"Why? I'm on vacation, remember? This is like camping in the woods; only with seaweed instead of poison ivy and bears."

That had ended that. Delaney had had to let it go. And so this time Tom really was on vacation. And Maggie could already see that this period of full relaxation was doing wonders for both his mental and physical health.

"What do you want to do tonight?" Maggie asked him, looking at him with a twinkle in her eyes.

"Evil woman, leave me alone."

She ignored his protests, and read from the ship's entertainment program from a brochure she picked up earlier in their room: "The options are: we can either go dancing to the disco music of Soul Bob's Popcorn Club, or . . ."

"No disco tonight. My belly already feels like it's dancing. Did you just say 'Popcorn Club?' "

"That's what it says in the program." She shrugged. "Okay, then, no disco tonight as grumpy husband has personal discotheque in belly . . ."

"Leave me alone."

". . . The other options are . . . Hey, here's one you're sure to like: 'Feel like you need to take the weight of the world off your feet? Then come to *Embers* and enjoy the seductive rhumba and samba sounds of the delightful Adriana Fernandez. Let the beautiful Brazilian jazz pianist relax both your body and soul with her incredible jazzy melodies and her smooth contralto voice and—' "

"Yeah, I think she'll do," Tom growled. "Now, darling, please stop talking and let me suffer in peace."

Maggie let him be. She already felt intrigued by the picture of the pianist. A pretty young woman with a wounded smile. She had a lot of suffering in her face; that was for certain.

Maggie began looking forward to hearing Adriana Fernandez play.

CHAPTER 24

The *Embers* lounge was about half full. As expected, given the sort of music the program advertised, most of the audience were in their later years. The younger musically-inclined passengers were more likely to be found dancing to hip-hop or rock in one of the other entertainment rooms.

Tom and Maggie sat in a pair of empty seats near the stage. This was because Maggie liked to watch musicians playing their instruments.

"It might be too loud," Tom protested, gesturing to the large array of loudspeakers on the stage, all fastened in place just like their seats in case the sea suddenly rocked the boat.

"Don't worry. I've already checked out the ship's acoustic treatments and they're state of the art. We're only sitting this close 'cos I want to watch her play."

"Ladies and gentlemen, may I present Miss Adriana Fernandez!"

"Well, at least she's pretty," Tom said with a laugh as the emcee left the stage and Adriana Fernandez walked on, dressed in a sleeveless yellow evening dress.

Maggie rolled her eyes and playfully nudged her husband. "Don't you start getting any ideas. Just listen, don't ogle."

"You sound worse than my mom."

Without any ado, Adriana bowed to the audience, sat behind a Yamaha electric piano and adjusted the microphone to the height of her lips.

"I think this is going to be very good," Maggie said, her voice dripping with anticipation.

And it was. Afterward, even Tom, who wasn't particularly musical, had to admit he'd been impressed. From the moment the young woman had first touched the piano keys, magic seemed to fill the air. Even songs both Tom and Maggie were familiar with took on a new lease of life beneath her fingers. She played Ella Fitzgerald and Louis Armstrong's *Cheek to Cheek*, singing both parts, Amy Winehouse's *Back to Black*, and several other standards and seemed to breathe new life into each one. And it wasn't the tunes themselves, it was all her. Half of the time the Brazilian girl had her eyes closed while playing and a rapturous look on her face that matched that of most of the audience as they listened to those old and familiar melodies made new by her incredible talent.

After the hour-and-a-half-long concert, the applause was unanimous.

"Wow, she was good," Maggie said as Adriana took a bow and played an encore, a song about the future that she'd written herself. The song was a good one, perfectly interpreted by Adriana's sultry contralto voice, though one could tell that she wasn't a trained singer.

A small crowd gathered around the singer, both to congratulate her on her playing and to just talk music. Maggie felt like joining them, but then changed her mind. All of a sudden Tom didn't look too good. Maggie could see that he was trying not to let his discomfort show.

After a wistful smile at the smiling young musician on the stage, Maggie pulled Tom to his feet. "C'mon, let's get you back to our cabin," she told him. "I can tell you're only doing this for me."

"I'm alright," he protested. "Go talk to her. I know you want to."

She shook her head. "Tomorrow will do just as well. She has several more performances throughout the week." Then she frowned. "Listen, darling, if by tomorrow you still don't feel good, we'll see the ship's doctor."

He nodded as he led the way out of the lounge.

CHAPTER 25

Thankfully, Tom's seasickness had cleared up by the next morning and they didn't need to see the doctor. After spending the day lounging about Costa Maya, their port of call that day, Tom suggested that they watch the 'Brazilian sensation' again that night.

So they did. This time though, Adriana Fernandez performed with a band made up of members of some of the other groups on the cruise.

Adriana was as incredible as on the previous night. Maggie felt she was listening at a once-in-a-lifetime talent.

However, Maggie had no chance to talk to the young woman tonight also, as Adriana left the stage half-way through the concert and the band finished the set without her.

But by now a plan—a crazy plan—had begun forming in Maggie's mind. Maggie was in awe of Adriana's talent and was thinking she could put it to better use than playing jazz standards on a cruise ship.

***

"I have to talk to that girl today," Maggie said, as she and Tom stood in the atrium of the ship's main deck—the fifth floor that served as a mini-mall of sorts—complete with a perfume shop, jewelry store, gift shop, liquor, and tobacco store—and connector to the CasaAqua's formal dining restaurant.

The two were in a large atrium admiring a glistening staircase that traversed several decks, where each step was transparent and embedded with hundreds, maybe thousands, of crystals, causing a dazzling spectacle of light from all directions.

Tom turned from starring at the Swarovski wonder to stare at his wife instead.

"What's so important about her?" he asked.

"I'm thinking of hiring her for our jazz club back home," she said.

At that statement Tom lost all interest in watching the ship's architecture. He turned, leaned on the railing and stared intently at his wife. "Honey, are you serious?"

She turned to him and nodded, then resumed staring out at the atrium.

Tom mused on that for a few moments. Maggie had 'that look' in her eyes, which meant she'd thought long and hard on this before consulting him about it.

Is she actually consulting me about it or just informing me of what the final outcome is going to be? Because if she's already made up her mind . . . He just managed not to sigh loudly. *I really don't need this complication now. I just want to get my head clear again; and this cruise has been working a treat and now this . . .*

Maggie didn't notice his inner conflict. She wasn't looking at him, anyway, instead still staring at the open atrium, its staircase, and the random guests on the varying decks coming and going. Whether intentionally or incidentally, Tom couldn't tell.

"Listen, darling, I didn't tell you about it earlier because I've only just made up my mind to speak to her," she went on.

Ah, she's made up her mind to hire the girl if she can. "Okay, I agree with you that she's talented enough . . ."

"She's as good as Jerry Bennet. If she was any more talented, she'd be receiving a Grammy award."

" . . . *But* can we afford her services?"

Maggie turned to look at him again, her eyes and face enthusiastic. "In this case, money comes second. First of all, I need to get her to say 'yes' to us."

Tom nodded. *Well, at least I don't have to be part of the negotiations; I just have to pay for the results.* "And here I was thinking this would be a simple uneventful vacation."

"Oh, don't be like that. You know I didn't plan for this to happen."

"It might not happen anyway. A talented girl like that has to be in demand elsewhere."

Maggie shook her head. "I'll bet you she's not. That's why she's playing on this cruise ship. You heard her accent; though her English is correct, it's completely unpolished, like she learnt it from TV. Darling, I think this is Adriana's first time of leaving Brazil. She's not a sensation yet simply because no one else but those of us on this ship know how good she is. And that is certain to change soon. That's why I need to talk to her now, before someone else with better music connections does." She looked at Tom narrowly. "Are you gonna support me on this, or what?"

He shrugged, staring up over her head at a distant elevator moving up on a wall behind the stairs. "Honey, you've got the final say on the club. It's always been that way."

"Yeah, but you'll be helping me pay her; and because of that I need you fully on board. I don't want you holding it against me for the next ten years."

"Oh, honey, have I *ever* held anything against you?"

She rolled her eyes at him. "Lots of times. Do you really want me to start naming specific instances?"

Tom laughed. "Oh alright, honey, go talk to the girl—what harm can it do?"

She beamed at him. "You really mean it?"

He nodded. "Yeah, what harm can it do?"

She leaned up on the rail and kissed him on the cheek. "Oh, thanks, I'll do so tonight. I checked the band schedule; she's playing in—" Then Maggie gave a yelp and froze. "Hey, there she is right now! And she's all alone."

Before Tom could say anything, Maggie had left him by the railing and dashed off along the deck. Tom stared after her for a moment. He couldn't see the Brazilian girl, just Maggie's red sundress vanishing around a corner.

Sighing again, he returned his attention to the sea. He opened the door that led to an open-air walking deck outside that circled the entirety of the ship. There were lifeboats anchored on this deck hoisted above the walking area, but it still afforded a nice view of the gulf and the Mexican coastline in the late afternoon. And, as a bonus, the lifeboats cast a shadow on the deck, making it comfortable and cool from the tropical sunshine. Soon, it would be sunset, and it would get much cooler once the ship picked up momentum and continued to its next port of call.

Two kids ran past him with their parents several paces behind trying to catch up. Tom smiled wistfully at them found himself wishing he and Maggie had been able to have children of their own. He looked up at the coast and then to a cloudbank overhead. The formation looked like a hill of melted marshmallows.

Tom was about to laugh at the corny simile when suddenly he got a splitting headache and his vision blanked out for a moment. It wasn't a total loss of sight, but everything around him suddenly lost its clear definition, till the people and objects around him all seemed like the images in a faded old portrait.

The pain in his head had him sagging against the railing, but he recovered himself before anyone noticed, gripping the railing to hold himself upright. Then the headache faded away and his vision sharpened again.

Darn it, I need a lot more rest! he thought. This was how it had been happening in his office: sudden sharp headaches that made his vision fade, and then the reverse case, the headaches faded, and his vision sharpened again. *It hasn't happened since I've been on the ship, but it also hasn't ever been as intense as this before, or lasted as long either.*

By now he could see clearly again. However, fearing a repeat of what had just happened to him, Tom didn't dare attempt the walk to he and Maggie's cabin. Instead, he trudged the few yards across to a deck chair beside a sleeping old woman and lowered himself down in it.

He shut his eyes and imagined all was well in his world. But he couldn't shake the feeling that something might be wrong with him, other than just the cumulative effects of too much computer usage.

CHAPTER 26

"Okay, mama, I'll be on my watch, but you really are worrying too much about this. Joao is long gone. And even if he wasn't, why would you ever imagine that he'd join a sea cruise when the police are looking for him?"

"I'm just saying to be careful," Bruna Fernandez said, her voice weak and squeaky because of the internet phone connection.

"Don't worry, mama, I will be," Adriana dutifully replied. "Do you still have enough money, or should I send you some more?"

"Yes, we do, darling. I just got a job helping out at Mr. Perez's bookstore and I've also taken up making hats again, so . . ."

They chatted for a while longer as Adriana climbed the stairs to Deck Seven. Things were much the same at home, mama said. The pandemic was mostly over, but things were just as hard as ever; and the greedy politicians were beginning to fill their pockets again. Hopefully the next elections will bring a fresh crop with young and honest blood, and not simply be another recycling and rotation of the same corrupt old guard.

Adriana said a silent prayer that such would be the case and then hung up.

She'd arrived at a small enclave near the *Embers* Lounge that starred out of a window on the ship's port side watching the sun disappear completely behind a Mexican landscape. She stood in solitude, trying to push down the fear caused by her mother's warning that Joao Ramires, not content with the misery he'd already caused in their lives, had vowed to 'get her' no matter how long it took him.

Yes, I told the police he shot Mario and Renato; but maybe it would have been better for us all if I'd kept my mouth shut, like most of the others at the club that night did. Then I wouldn't need to keep looking over my shoulder all the time because some crazy man wants me out of the way. According to mama, even Renato's brother Tomás—

"Hey there, is it okay if I join you for a little while?"

The voice startled Adriana out of her thoughts. At first, she was frightened that true to her mother's own concerns, the fugitive Joao Ramires had found her on the ship and was about to exact his terrifying revenge. But it was just another passenger, an American woman whom she had noticed at several of her performances over the past few days. Both times the woman had been accompanied by a man that Adriana assumed was her husband.

"I'm sorry if I startled you," the woman said. "I would have spoken to you downstairs, but you were on the phone and I didn't want to interrupt your conversation."

Adriana smiled. "That's okay. I was just telling my old mother in Brazil not to worry so much about me."

The woman smiled back and nodded. "Is there somewhere up here where we can sit and chat? I need to discuss something with you."

Bemused, Adriana nodded and led the way over to a set of secluded chairs normally reserved for cruise staff use.

***

Once they were seated, the American woman spoke and Adriana listened. As she listened, she became more and more surprised.

". . . So, my husband and I are wondering if you'd consider taking up a residency at out little club, the Jazzy Truth."

Adriana was very interested. She'd always dreamed of living and working in America, the country where the world's most famous musicians came from. But still, she was cautious. She knew she was good-looking, and even though this pleasant middle-aged American woman—Maggie Duchensky—didn't look it, she and her husband might merely be recruiting for a prostitution ring. One of Adriana's own nightmares (added to by her mother's fear of such a thing happening to her) was of being caught and trafficked in some black-market slave trade.

Of course, this didn't seem to be the case here; Mrs. Duchensky had shown her the club's website, along with videos of musicians playing there. The music was all jazz; dark and earthy music that tugged at Adriana's heartstrings, calling to her to emigrate at once and seek the mecca of music.

But still . . . lots of things were too good to be true. One could never be too careful with strangers.

She played it cool. "I'll be lying if I say I'm uninterested," Adriana replied, hoping her English was correct. Her English had improved greatly while she'd been working the cruise, but she still felt uncertain of her pronunciation when addressing its native speakers. "But . . . even if I do agree to work with you, I can't leave the cruise yet. I've still got two months left on my contract."

Maggie smiled. "That's no problem at all; you can join us when your contract is up. All Tom and I are asking at the moment is that you seriously consider our offer. Like I said, we'll match what you're earning now, plus you'll have free accommodation in one of the two apartments above the club. Also, you'll have some things I doubt the cruise covers, like health insurance coverage and access to a retirement plan. In addition, Wheeling is a lovely town. They have a symphony orchestra there and it's very close to Pittsburgh. You're certain to enjoy living there. The Jazzy Truth is situated in a great neighborhood, and you'll have lots of free time to pursue your own interests."

A cold sea breeze blew over them both then and Adriana's companion turned to stare at an outward-facing door that someone had just opened and came inside. Then she went on: "If you do decide to be our resident musician, we'll offer you a six-month contract at first and we can renegotiate after that. Even if you don't like our place, working there for six months should give you sufficient time to make the musical connections to move on to somewhere else. All Tom and I are asking at the moment, is that you let us know once you decide, so we can begin working on stuff like your immigration status and your

American work permit. It's the month of March now. I'd love to have you in the US by July."

Adriana nodded. "I'll definitely think about it, Maggie. One can't be a lounge act forever."

"No, one can't." Maggie agreed, laughing.

The woman's laughter was warm and pure, and Adriana felt drawn to her.

With negotiations out of the way, their discussion now turned to other things: Music in general, musicians in particular, and then life, with all of its ups and downs. Maggie shared incidences of her life with Adriana, who was particularly touched by the couple's inability to have children. She in turn shared her own experiences with Maggie.

"Oh, I'm so sorry to hear it," Maggie said when she told her about the club shooting that had put her brother in a wheelchair. And Adriana could tell that the other woman's empathy was genuine; she really did sympathize with her.

Suddenly, Adriana realized that she'd found a good friend. This American woman that she'd just met and who was trying to employ her, seemed to be someone she could unburden herself to.

"Hey, come on," Maggie said finally, rising to her feet. "It's getting to about dinnertime. Let's go find my husband and all have dinner together."

Feeling very happy, Adriana got to her feet too, and followed her new friend downstairs.

PART THREE:
BACK IN THE USA
(THREE MONTHS LATER)

CHAPTER 27

"Yes, mama, I also think I'm living in a dream," Adriana said and cut the connection.

After a glance around her bedroom, she dropped the cell phone in her purse and left the apartment.

The two apartments above the Jazzy Truth club were accessed by a stairway that ran down the left side of the building to the rear. This design was apparently to prevent club patrons becoming confused as to which entrance to head for once they left the parking lot. Around the rear of the building, there was sufficient parking space for four cars.

Adriana's apartment was the further one. To reach the stairs, she had to walk past Eddie the bartender's place.

As she descended the stairs, Adriana noticed both Eddie's old brown hatchback and Maggie's blue SUV parked in the rear lot. She hoped to have a car of her own soon. She had her mind set on something small, but elegant and ladylike.

Halfway down the external staircase, Adriana paused and looked out over her new neighborhood.

No, Maggie didn't lie. This is a great place to live in! I feel like I'm one step away from heaven!

One thing that had immediately struck Adriana on arriving here in West Virginia was how much space there was.

The situation of the Jazzy Truth was a case in point. The club existed in a giant parking lot (well, 'giant' to Adriana's previously cramped perspective) with a generous allotment of trees on either side. On the left, the next building was fifty yards away; on the right, one walked a short distance to the connecting street. This section of town wasn't as busy, but if you drove the street a few blocks down, you would see several storefronts and the Capitol Music Hall.

Before joining the CasaAqua cruise, Adriana had lived in cramped spaces for her entire life. In her mind she was used to residential situations where people practically lived on top of each other. Having this much space around her was going to take some getting used to. Yes, she knew that in lots of American cities (which she hoped to visit soon) the housing situation was almost as cramped as it was back home in Belém; but one wouldn't know it from living here in the Mountain State.

Maggie had mentioned that West Virginia's motto was "Almost Heaven." In fact, she had pointed it out on a road sign as they crossed the state line driving from the Pittsburgh International Airport into West Virginia. Adriana had genuinely hoped that to be the case.

Suddenly, triggered by her thoughts of home, Adriana remembered Mario. Oftentimes, just like this, seemingly out of the blue, dark thoughts of her dearly departed brother came to torment her. But when this happened, she did her best to be strong.

Now, she choked back the tears that automatically followed the memories and consoled herself, telling herself that the past was the past, that Mario was dead now; dead and gone and there was nothing to be gained from endlessly mourning him. All she could do now was press forward into the future and do her best to build a good life for both herself and her poor mother back home in Belém.

Once she felt properly in control of herself again, Adriana continued her descent and finally walked around to the front of the club building. She could have entered the club by its rear entrance, but this afternoon she felt like stretching her legs a little.

Visible from the club entrance, across the street were a grocery shop and a liquor store. Adriana crossed the parking lot to the sidewalk and stood watching while several cars drove past. Then she turned and walked back to the club.

Maggie was waiting for her at the club entrance.

"Have a good night?" her employer asked.

Adriana nodded enthusiastically. "Just great, thanks."

Maggie pulled the door open and stepped back inside. "Come in, let's discuss tomorrow night."

Adriana followed her inside, and together they walked over to the bar, where Eddie was tidying up.

The two women sat on bar stools and Maggie snapped her fingers to get Eddie's attention. "Coffees for both of us," she told him.

"Coming right up!" came the cheerful reply.

Adriana liked Eddie. He was younger than she was and very friendly. She was fast becoming friends with Eddie's girlfriend Traci as well. Music-wise, Eddie was a good drummer and when they jammed together with his friend Eric on the sax, their improvised trio sounded good. Not great, but no one was complaining.

"Okay," Maggie said. "Fill me in some more on this Tolbert kid you've got coming over from Akron?"

Adriana shrugged. "I met him via Facebook. He's seventeen and a really good guitarist, plays very mature for his age. Think Carlos Santana in a jazz context and you can't go wrong."

"Santana? Wow, he must be good then."

Adriana nodded, enthused as always once music was the subject under discussion. "He's great. Another thing is—he's not charging us for having him. He just wants to jam with me; and maybe record a few songs live for both our portfolios. He'll be staying in town for two weeks."

Eddie placed their steaming coffees in front of them. "I told him he can stay in my apartment, and that we'd feed him too," he told Maggie.

Maggie nodded. "Feeding the kid won't be a problem. If he's as good as you say, we'll even give him some cash when he's leaving."

"That's what I thought," Adriana said. "Anyhow, he'll be in town tomorrow morning. Meanwhile, Eddie and I have been working on setting up the video recording equipment for the live streaming."

"Yeah," Eddie agreed. "I picked up a streaming compatible DSLR from Best Buy. I think it will work well for our shows. Traci is the one who recommended it after finding it was on sale." Eddie's girlfriend Traci would be overseeing the video recordings.

The trio chatted on, getting things ready for the next night. After a while a few drinking patrons wandered in, and Adriana and Maggie left the bar to the barflies and retreated to a quiet corner of the room to continue their preparations.

"So how do you like the USA so far?" Maggie asked.

"I totally love it!" Adriana enthusiastically replied. "It's everything I expected it would be—the people, the environment . . . the music . . ."

And it was true. She looked over to the stage, at the upright piano and Fender Rhodes that she'd played on every night since her arrival here two weeks ago. She already felt an intense fondness for the instruments. Despite the shortness of time that she'd been here, she felt like this was her turf now; this club and these people and this jazz music. She felt as committed to making things work here as Maggie was.

And her friendship with Maggie had continued to blossom. When she'd left Brazil for the second time to come to America, Adriana had been scared by horror stories she'd heard about other émigrés, her term for describing immigrants; people who'd also left for the greener pastures that the world's greatest nation represented, only to find themselves working virtually as slaves—menial laborers in sweatshops, or maids and worse than that—with their passports seized by their supposed American benefactors. Her mother in particular had heard every variation of horror story imaginable. Aided by gossip and the internet, Bruna Fernandez had an incredibly fertile imagination where the abuse of Brazilian émigrés was concerned.

A huge amount of that fear had transmitted itself to her daughter.

And yet, it's been nothing at all like that, Adriana realized. *Maggie's been almost like a substitute mother to me. No, not a mother—she's the loving and caring older sister I've always wanted and never had. I'm in absolutely no danger here with her and her husband. Maggie acts as if she'd protect me with her own life, if necessary.*

She smiled at Maggie, as the older woman called Eddie over to check that they had enough drinks in storage to cater to tomorrow night's anticipated turnout of concert goers.

Even her husband Tom seems to like me. He's reserved though. I can tell that he doesn't trust me yet. He thinks I'm taking advantage of his wife, or that I'm going to someday; that I'm only here to use them as stepping stones to something better the moment it comes. But that's not the case. My motives in coming here are both honest and pure, and I'm certain that in time Mr. Duchensky will recognize that too.

"Well, I believe we're good to go," Maggie said finally. "So long as you and Eddie get the streaming setup working before showtime, everything should work out fine."

Adriana nodded. "We'll have everything ready on time. You'll see."

CHAPTER 28

"So, I gotta ask: where the hell did you find that kid?" Tom asked.

"Which kid?"

"That guitarist who looks like he ran away from home last week."

"Oh, you mean Tolbert?"

Tom nodded.

It was Saturday morning. After beginning the day with a passionate bout of lovemaking, Tom and Maggie were relaxing against one another. His head was up on a pillow; her head was on his chest. Tom felt good about the world; sex with Maggie always did that to him, made him feel like he could singlehandedly fix all of existence's problems.

Maggie giggled and looked up at him. "Why? Do you think he's good?" Then she slapped his bare chest with a hand. "Hey, if you're asking about Tolbert, that means you streamed last night's performance on YouTube like I asked you to."

Tom laughed. "Well, hon, you more-or-less threatened me with a month's worth of abstinence if I didn't. So, I took a few minutes break from my endless overtime and had a peek." His voice turned serious. "But, wow, that boy can play guitar. I wish I could play guitar like that."

Maggie patted him playfully again. "Best you stick to coding data, darling—it's what you do best. Besides, remember what they say about wishes and horses."

Tom made a face. "Yeah, I guess you're right. How's business going tho'? Club seemed full last night."

"It was. Our first standing room only crowd in close to a year."

"How'd you get so many people anyway?"

"It was Adriana's work. She and Tolbert got going on Instagram and TikTok like you wouldn't believe. Apparently, the kid's got quite a following. You'd have noticed that a lot of the audience were youngsters themselves. From what we heard, a good number of the kids are staying the weekend with friends in town just to watch him play again tonight. Hey, you aren't workin' tonight are you? Why not come down and watch him play? Drinks on the house as usual."

"Oh, I'd never pay to drink in that terrible dive of yours."

"You never will, cheapskate. That's why you married the owner."

Tom laughed. "Yeah. But, yeah, I think I'll check the music out tonight. See if I can't interest some of the guys from work too."

Happy, Maggie snuggled up close to Tom and he draped his arm around her and pulled up the sheet over her shoulders.

Tom felt glad that his wife's gamble on the unknown Brazilian girl was paying off. He'd more than had his reservations while she'd insisted on 'importing' Adriana from Brazil like a can of exotic coffee. But Maggie had insisted and persisted and 'voila!' here was the fruit of her labor: Adriana Fernandez living and working in the USA.

And hopefully making us enough money to pay her wages.

But even this was merely a joke thought. Tom suspected Maggie's new friend and protégé would prove worth her weight in gold. In fact, Maggie's investment in bringing Adriana to America had already begun paying dividends. The girl had been here less than a month and Tom already found himself pulling less hours of overtime because of the money the Jazzy Truth had resumed making.

He also liked the way the two women had bonded and become close friends. Before Adriana's coming, Maggie hadn't really been close to anyone, but now . . . Tom liked seeing how she smiled when Adriana was coming over to the house.

"What are you thinking about?" Maggie asked.

"Huh?" Tom looked down at her and saw the speculative look on her face.

"I'm just thinking about us," he replied honestly. "I'm thinking that if things carry on like this with the club, in a month I'll be able to stop doing so much overtime and punch out at five p.m. like everyone else does, and then we can spend our evenings together like we used to."

Maggie giggled and squeezed closer to him. "Um, I'd really like that. We see each other so little during the week now. Sometimes I almost want us to go on another cruise just so we can spend more time together."

Tom laughed. "Delaney won't like it."

"I don't care what Delaney likes. What *I* like is what counts here, and— Honey, what's the matter?"

Tom had just felt that splitting headache again and his face showed his pain, his lips warped up into a grimace. "It's that—"

"Did your eyesight fade out again like the previous times?" Maggie asked in concern.

Tom nodded and gently rolled her off of him. Then he sat on the side of bed and gently cradled his head in his hands. "Yeah, it did, but I'm okay now."

Tom had said this simply to calm Maggie. He couldn't really see clearly now, but his vision was returning; both his wife and the objects in their bedroom seeming to be coming back into existence again. The problem was, that unlike previously, when the headaches and the disruption of his eyesight coincided exactly, now sometimes Tom had no warning at all—all of a sudden he'd been unable to see for a few seconds. It always passed, but it was scary as hell while it lasted.

"I've an appointment to see the optometrist about it on Monday," he told Maggie, seeking to further reassure her. "I'm long overdue for fresh reading glasses."

She looked unconvinced and Tom understood why. He'd been due to see the eye doctor ever since they'd returned from the cruise, but had kept putting it off. He knew why that was: he was frightened of discovering he'd need to take time off from work to attend to his vision. Yes, Tom realized he needed 20/20 vision to do his IT job right, but he didn't have the time to take off; they'd needed every cent he could earn.

But now . . .

"Listen, darling," Maggie said gently. "I know you're worried about our bills, but please understand that with me, your health comes first. Just go visit the doctor, huh? Even if your eyes need surgery and you have to take time off from work, we'll pull through somehow. We're lucky that this is coming right when the club is getting back on its feet again, so we've got some extra income coming in."

Tom nodded then leaned over and kissed her tenderly on the lips. "Thanks, hon. I'm glad that I can count on you. Don't worry, this time I really will go and see the optometrist."

CHAPTER 29

Tom did attend that night's performance at the club.

He was surprised at the turnout; once again, like the previous night, the crowd was standing room only, most of the space behind the tables occupied by a throng of youthful bodies that jostled for space. Yet more kids in denim and shaggy hair lined the bar with their drinks in hand. The place smelled of sweat and sweet perfume, as there were almost as many young women as young men in attendance.

Maggie had thoughtfully reserved a table for both of them near the stage.

"This has the ambience of a rock concert," Tom told her as the musicians walked on stage.

"Yeah, amazing, isn't it?" Her eyes shone with an excitement Tom hadn't seen in them for a long time. He was glad she was so happy. For so long their conversations had been depressing ones, and now Maggie was enthused about life again. Tom felt delighted for her.

Maggie left him to announce the band. "Good evening, ladies and gentlemen. Benny Green once said, 'A jazz musician is a juggler who uses harmonies instead of oranges.' Well, we don't have any oranges here except those in our drinks. So, once more tonight—and by popular demand, I might add—the Jazzy Truth presents to you Tolbert Hawes!

The applause was deafening. "So, let's all enjoy some jazz, folks!"

Maggie stood there on stage for a moment with a smile on her face and then rejoined Tom at the table. True to his word, Tom had called around his friends and invited them to the gig, but in most cases his notice was too short. However, one couple had said they'd make it; which was why there were two empty places at their table.

The band was comprised of four people: Adriana, Eddie, Eric the saxophone player, and Tolbert, with Adriana doubling up on piano and vocals.

The music began, and even Tom, who wasn't really musical, had to admit it was great. And tonight, listening live to the players, rather than over his Bluetooth earphones, he quickly realized something: that it was Adriana Fernandez, and not Tolbert who was the real star here, the MVP as they say in the sports leagues.

Yes, young Tolbert Hawes was an incredible jazz guitarist, someone deservedly regarded as a virtuoso and a clear star for the future, but it was Adriana's backing on the electric piano that enabled him to shine as he did tonight. Her playing was perfect; sublime and yet sophisticated; blending in with the other players and yet unmissable. And yet, she wasn't grandstanding, wasn't showing off. In fact, Adriana seemed totally unaware of the effect she was creating with her amazing talent. She sat there in her blue jeans and pink tee shirt, with a smile on her face and her black hair falling well below her shoulders, and those glorious chords and melodies streamed like magic from her long fingers.

Yes, Tom was very impressed.

During a break between numbers, Maggie leaned over him and whispered: "Adriana's fantastic, isn't she?"

"Oh, she's incredible. I can't tell when last I saw someone play this well."

Maggie made a face. "That's because you always leave the running of the club to me. Darling, we live just down the road and yet you're never here."

"That'll hopefully change soon," Tom said. Then his eyes widened. "Hey, Mick and Debbie just arrived."

He leapt to his feet, and waved to his friends, who, being middle-aged themselves, looked rather bemused at all the youngsters in the club.

While Adriana began singing a ballad about a lost-and-found love, Tom walked over to greet Mick and Debbie and usher them to their seats by the stage.

PART FOUR:
SERIOUS MISFORTUNE

CHAPTER 30

"And so, Mr. Duchensky, I'm sorry to inform you that what you have is incurable."

Incurable! The doctor's words rang like a bell in Tom's head as he sat in the living room watching TV. *How the hell can I be incurable? One little word and my life comes crashing down . . . for good.*

Tom's fall had begun the same way an avalanche did, like a single displaced rock trickling down the side of a mountain and dislodging other, larger rocks as it rolled along on its careless way, with those rocks, in turn, dislodging others, until that whole side of the mountain became a deadly cascade of falling stone.

Tom's initial visit to the optometrist had seen him referred to a specialist, which had resulted in him being subjected to a barrage of scans and tests, the extent of which baffled him.

"But we need to be absolutely certain," Dr. Hollis had afterward said and then sent him back for yet more tests. Medical insurance had covered the tests, but the test results had been damning.

"Mr. Duchensky, you have a tumor. An inoperable tumor growing in and bridging your visual cortexes. Dr. Hollis had tapped the back of Tom's head with a pencil. "Right here, in your occipital lobes, where your vision is controlled."

He walked around to Tom's front again and sat on the edge of his desk facing him. "This tumor is what has been causing your headaches and loss of vision. The bad news is that you're going blind. The really bad news is that the tumor will eventually kill you, either before or after you completely lose your vision, most likely at the same time."

"But can't you operate?" Maggie had asked. Not trusting himself in this situation, Tom had Maggie accompany him to the doctor's office that fateful morning. "Surely, with all of the modern surgical advances, you can cut the tumor out of him," she'd insisted.

Dr. Hollis nodded. "Yes, Mrs. Duchensky, we can operate on your husband; but doing so will do him no good. The tumor is just too integrated."

"I don't understand," Maggie had said. "Can you be clearer about this?"

"Yes, please, clarify this, doctor," Tom had agreed.

"The problem," Dr. Hollis explained, "is that successfully removing the tumor will also remove a good portion of the surrounding brain tissue, essential nerve tissue which the brain needs to function properly." He'd looked squarely at Maggie. "Once this tissue has been removed, your husband will be nothing more than a vegetable, completely unable to think or to move; and of course, removing the tumor would have already blinded him." He'd frowned. "I'm not trying to be insensitive, but in my opinion, death is preferable to such a fate, where one is technically dead but is still classified as being among the living."

Tom and Maggie had both gasped at the doctor's words, and Maggie had gripped Tom's hand hard and burst into tears.

They'd asked for a second and then a third opinion, but the prognosis was exactly the same. There was absolutely no cure for what Tom had.

Tom Duchensky was living on borrowed time.

***

This evening Maggie was over at the Jazzy Truth, so Tom sat alone in his living room and pondered his future.

What future? I don't have one anymore, do I?

Scouring both the internet and library for medical literature, Tom and Maggie had read up everything they could find on Tom's condition. Everything they'd read simply confirmed the doctors' words. Yes, what Tom had was extremely rare, and yes, there was no cure. In every case they read about, the sufferers had died, several by their own hands as their disease progressed in severity.

Tom didn't feel suicidal yet, just extremely downcast.

I think that's because I can still see, though my vision is fading more regularly now, coming and going like God is flicking my light switch on and off.

He looked at the laptop on the coffee table and as if on cue, his vision faded, rendering the entire living room a gray blur, a mess of erased off-white smears.

Tom felt no panic while waiting for the world to reappear around him; he just felt desolate. This happened at least once a day now; sometimes twice or even thrice. He knew what was happening; knew that it would soon end. But he also knew that it would repeat over and over again, with shorter intervals between occurrences of his seeing nothing. Until one day, the world would fade from view around him and would never come back into focus again.

The doctors had been unable to predict how long it would be before he was completely blind.

"Maybe a month from now, maybe six months. A year at most, if you're lucky," Dr. Hollis had said.

In time—the blinded man calculated the interval to about six minutes—the world reappeared around Tom again.

Heaving a sigh of relief, he pulled the laptop towards him and logged on remotely to his office's server.

***

At the moment, Tom was still able to work from home, but this arrangement would only last until his retirement packet had been completely organized.

Even his old work nemesis, his boss Delaney, had been shocked to discover that Tom was going blind. Tom hadn't let them know that he was dying too. He had his pride and didn't want any public effusions of pity.

Similarly, he'd not told his older sister Sharon or any of their other close relatives yet. (Just like with Maggie, both of his parents were already dead.) Everyone would find out in due course. Part of his reticence to pass on the information to his older sister was the aforementioned desire to not become an object of family pity; but there was also the additional factor that Tom himself hadn't yet fully come to terms with his lack of a future.

It's hard to sit here, feeling in the prime of good health and accept such a damning truth; that in a year's time, at most a year and a half, I'll be dead. Gone for good.

Tom had never been a religious man. Had he been religious, he might have prayed to God for miraculous intervention; or been angry at with God for disappointing him with this horrible illness after half-a-lifetime's faithful service. But not being a praying man, his interpretation of what was happening to him was 'what will be, will be.'

He didn't hold the Almighty responsible for his current misfortune. The only thing he blamed was his own faulty genes.

Of course, not blaming God didn't mean he didn't feel bitter. His anger visited at random times, often at times like this, when Maggie was down at the jazz club and he was left all alone in the house with the TV on, and time on his hands. Tom had quickly realized that an idle mind truly is the devil's workshop.

Staring at the TV, like he was doing now, watching all the healthy people who would continue being healthy long after he was dead and gone, was depressing to the core. The fact that lots of these healthy people were a lot older than he was just made it worse.

With this depression came anger.

He got to his feet, and kicked the coffee table. Then he stamped through the living room and front foyer to the front door. He opened the door and stepped outside the house. It was drizzling outside. He stood on the front porch imagining the clouds in the sky were his brains, and the rain was his sanity falling to the ground; his vision, his consciousness and personality drizzling away; till finally there was nothing left.

He felt it was an apt and extremely depressing comparison.

He looked left, down the road in the direction of the club. It would be the easiest thing in the world to pick up an umbrella and walk down there, to be with Maggie. Tom considered doing so, but then changed his mind. He felt mired in inertia, his feet stuck in the mud of existence; his drive to be more than what he currently was all but exhausted. And in addition, he didn't want to visit the club tonight because he suspected Maggie might not want him there.

Maggie probably spends so much time down at the club nowadays just to be away from me. I know I'm depressing her, but I don't know how I can stop it. If anything, she's taken the news of my illness and approaching demise worse than I have. And it's spilling over into our daily lives. We're slowly drifting apart from one another. I wonder what's next: sleeping in separate beds . . . separation . . . divorce?

A car turned the nearby corner, its headlights swinging suddenly into view and then away again.

Tom stood on the porch for a while longer, staring out into the rain and trying to get a hold of his negative emotions. After a while, when he felt his bitterness had subsided enough, he backed into the house, shut the door in the face of the rain, and retreated back to his couch and his lonely vigil with the television.

CHAPTER 31

Since waking up this Wednesday morning, Adriana had felt slightly apprehensive. She'd had no reason to feel so, but she knew feelings were unreasonable creatures, irrational emotional beasts that would dog one at the slightest hint of a departure from normality.

Now, while having lunch with Maggie, Adriana thought she knew why she'd been feeling apprehensive. The two of them were seated at an exterior table at a coffee shop in the local mall. She and Maggie had planned this shopping trip yesterday. There was a gig tonight at the club and Adriana wanted a new dress, while Maggie wanted to buy some new shoes.

They'd already completed their shopping and were eating lunch before driving back to the Jazzy Truth club. Their table had a parasol, which was nice because it was drizzling. Both their shopping bags and their handbags were off the floor, placed on chairs so they didn't become soaked.

While they had been shopping, something in Maggie's voice had filled Adriana with apprehension that she had something unpleasant to talk about. Adriana had even briefly flirted with the idea that Maggie was going to tell her that she couldn't keep working at the club, which would be a disaster, as she'd come to regard the Jazzy Truth as her 'home away from home.' So yes, she'd been steeling herself for unpleasant news.

But she'd not expected to hear *this*: *Tom is going blind? And he's also dying? Oh, my God, no!*

"But why didn't you . . . I mean, why haven't you said anything about it to me before now?" Adriana asked.

"I wanted to. I really did. But I didn't mention it to you because Tom has his pride, and he doesn't want people to know about his illness just yet," Maggie explained with tears in her eyes. "The tumor's effect is still intermittent and only impairs his vision occasionally. You know that at the moment Tom can still see quite well. But soon . . ." She pulled a handkerchief from her purse and dabbed her eyes.

Adriana reached across the small table and gripped Maggie's hands. "Oh, I'm so sorry to hear this. I'd like to do something to help. What can I do?"

Maggie smiled. "Just understanding is enough."

Adriana smiled back. But then Maggie broke down completely in tears.

"Oh, I don't know if I can take this anymore," she wept pitifully. "I understand that men have their pride, and yes, Tom is no different from other men, but . . . Since the doctors passed their death sentence on him . . . Tom seems to have become a different person. He's so distant now that sometimes I feel that I'm living alone, even though we sleep in the same bed and eat at the same table."

Adriana kept her face impassive. With her own past experiences of misfortunes, she felt she understood what Maggie was going through. But of course, no two situations were ever exactly the same.

This must be how mama felt when daddy dropped dead of that heart attack. Or maybe how I felt when Mario was run down by that drunken driver.

Oh, Mario. For a moment her throat constricted as she remembered him.

As for Tom, she didn't know what to think. She wasn't as close to him as she was to Maggie. She liked him, but the feeling wasn't exactly mutual. Though Tom Duchensky had always been polite and very nice to her, she continually sensed a wall of reservation emanating from him, although recently he seemed to be softening towards her. And there was also the factor that because he was a man, a close relationship between the two of them might not really be desirable.

Being too friendly with Tom can easily lead to all kinds of misconceptions, both on his part and on mine; and what about Maggie's own feelings? So maybe it's best the way things have been between Tom and me. If the two of us had become close friends, how long would it be before Maggie might begin suspecting that there's something more happening between us? And that would cripple my friendship with Maggie, a friendship that I value more than just about anything right now.

But the fact that Tom was her best friend's husband made his current fatal affliction of grave importance to Adriana. Such was Adriana's commitment to Maggie Duchensky that whatever affected Maggie affected Adriana personally. Adriana was a straightforward person. Since arriving in America, she had never felt anything other than gratitude and respect for the couple who'd helped her come here; and had never had any other desire than to do the job she'd been hired to do as well as she possibly could, and so help put the Jazzy Truth back on the music map once more. And if by doing so, she progressed herself, all well and good. But if not, then so be it.

Because, in addition to being a nice and a humble soul, Adriana Fernandez truly had no idea how good a musician she was.

"I think the main problem Tom has now is one of identity," Maggie explained, while Adriana listened intently, feeling as if her own heart was breaking along with her friend's.

"How do you mean, identity?" she asked, while around them the drizzle waxed and waned.

Maggie dabbed her eyes dry again before replying: "Ever since I've known, Tom, he's been proud of his job. I mean in the sense that he completely identifies with it. For him being an IT professional is who he is—that's what I mean by identity. Tom and his job are one and the same; take away one of them and the other ceases to exist."

Adriana thought that she got it: "And now that he's losing his vision . . ."

"Exactly," Maggie went on. "Now that my husband's eyesight is failing, it's the same thing as *himself* failing—not as in his health failing, even though it is, but in himself failing both as a man and a human being. Of course, if he was just being laid off due to budget cutbacks, it wouldn't be half as bad; he could just shop around for another job, but with his vision going, he clearly can't work in IT anymore, meaning in his mind he's essentially been rendered completely useless."

"That's just horrible," Adriana said sincerely. She felt a horror at the thought. For her it would be the same thing as having her fingers cut off, so she couldn't play the piano again. What would she do then?

I'd commit suicide, she realized.

Maggie smiled sadly. "The worst part of this is—I don't think Tom even realizes that that's what the problem is. It's up to me to point it out to him, but what is the point of my doing so?"

"He could see a therapist instead. Maybe that will help him."

Maggie nodded and then shook her head emphatically. "I guess it would, but no, Tom won't ever go to see a therapist. If I suggested it to him, he'll point out to me, and rightly so I admit, 'What's the use?' We both know he's dying anyway—what's the use of wasting money when he'll probably be dead in a year?"

Maggie began weeping again. At a loss for words, Adriana remembered her lunch and picked at it. For her part, Maggie's food was uneaten; her coffee undrunk. After a few mouthfuls of salad, Adriana asked: "So, what are you going to do now?"

She didn't expect the reply she got:

"I'm thinking of leaving Tom," Maggie said bluntly, with a frigid look on her face, and her shoulders squared as if she was carrying a huge burden on them. "I've already consulted a divorce lawyer and they'll serve Tom the divorce papers anytime I feel like doing so."

"No, you can't do that," Adriana immediately objected. "That'll be a cruel thing to do to him."

The square set of Maggie's shoulders instantly collapsed again. "That's just the problem," she admitted, much to Adriana's relief. "I know I can't just leave Tom to his own mess. Not right now when I know he needs me more than ever. But . . ." More tears ran down her cheeks, as if she was raining on the inside. "But, our relationship is so strained now, that I've no idea what else I can do, even though I do love him."

She peered intently at Adriana. "Oh yes, I still love Tom with all of my heart, but . . . it's like living with a stranger now. Our relationship seems to have crumbled to nothing; burnt to ashes, or maybe"—and then her gaze snagged off to the left, tracking a woman in a raincoat, and she gestured vaguely beyond the woman at the shops and the shoppers—"maybe our once rock-solid relationship has simply melted away and become mud under the force of life's storms."

Adriana had no immediate reply to this. She once more reached across the table and took Maggie's hands in hers. She said nothing and Maggie wept for a while, until finally Maggie asked: "I'm at a total loss now, Adriana. I need your advice. What do you think I should do? What would you do in my situation?"

"I'd remain with Tom," Adriana promptly replied. "Despite how hard things are between you both at the moment, I'd remain by Tom's side and support him through this. Because . . ." she paused and gazed into Maggie's eyes, trying to make her older friend feel what she felt, "because I think that's what Tom would do for you. He'd remain by your side until the bitter end, no matter how long it took. And, Maggie, if you truly do love your husband, you've no choice but to do the same for him. You need to stay by his side and love him all the way through this, till the moment of his death."

Adriana had no idea what the effect of her words would be. For a moment Maggie's eyes flared up in visible anger and rebellion, and Adriana thought they were about having a heated argument. But then the anger just as visibly died in Maggie and she smiled. It was a sad smile, but Adriana felt certain that the danger of desertion and divorce were past.

She was right. Maggie said, "Thanks, I really needed to hear this. And now I know that you understand, it'll be a whole lot easier for me to deal with."

Adriana nodded. "Yes, I'm here for you both. Just let me know whatever I can do to help."

Maggie nodded and began weeping again. But this time her eyes were filled with hopeful tears, tears of courageous resolve.

Adriana pointed to Maggie's untouched lunch. "Unless you mind trying one of Eddie's overcooked hamburgers back at the club, try to eat something. We'll be busy the whole afternoon."

Maggie dried her eyes again and then ate her lunch.

CHAPTER 32

The rest of the afternoon passed swiftly. Adriana and Eddie did a brief soundcheck with Rory Davis, the out-of-town saxophone player who was tonight's featured musical attraction. Rory was old and jovial, a white-haired muso who'd been hawking his music everywhere since the days of disco; along the way, he'd even recorded and played concerts with both Sun-Ra and Chick Corea. Adriana felt honored to be playing along such a seasoned great, and when she and Rory began comparing notes about music, she quickly realized there was a whole lot she could learn from the old man during his short stint here at the Jazzy Truth.

Rory was easy-going to the core; a few beers and he began telling stories of life on the road that alternatively had Adriana blushing and roaring with laughter.

"Oh, li'l missy," Rory laughed. "You need to have seen the look on Kenny's face when he woke up the next morning stark naked in the pig pen, covered in mud and with piglets sleeping on him. Rest assured, he never drunk rum again after that night!"

Adriana, Eddie, and the drinkers at the bar all howled with laughter.

Several times that afternoon, Adriana locked eyes with Maggie as they each went about their business. Each time Maggie would smile back at her. There was a peace in Maggie's eyes now that reassured her Brazilian employee that she would stick to her word to stand by Tom's side during his crisis.

Adriana still hadn't yet come to terms with exactly how terminal Tom's sickness was. *Last time I saw him, he looked as healthy as ever! But he's dying? He might not last another year?*

It was terrifying to consider. Adriana fully understood Maggie's reluctance to remain in such a situation, particularly after she'd described the unexpected toxicity that now simmered between herself and her husband. But Adriana had been brought up to expect lovers—married and otherwise—to stick together through thick and thin. What was the proof of their love for one another if they didn't? What was love worth if it couldn't weather life's storms? In such cases the so-called lovers were no better than fair-weather friends.

So it was that the afternoon passed, and night came.

CHAPTER 33

Eddie laid down a solid swing beat, all hi-hats and kick drum. Adriana played a jagged chord progression full of ascent and descent, and old Rory Davis blew the saxophone. Or maybe it was more accurate to say Rory 'blue' the sax. From the moment Rory started playing his horn, there was stupefied silence in the club. Once more, everyone present—mostly old-timers like the saxophonist himself—understood that they were in the presence of greatness. For sure, the player might be old, but the game went on.

Adriana relaxed and gave her all to the music. She felt it flow through her veins like her blood, felt it pulse in her temples like the beat of Eddie's kick drum. She felt each consonance and dissonance they played thrill in her soul like a primeval beast lurking in the swamps of New Orleans.

The music was all—and she gave it her all. At least she did so until the club door swung open and Joao Ramires walked in.

Adriana instinctively froze, her fingers stopping short on the keyboard. She'd stopped at a good place, however; just as Eddie was about to take a short drum break, and so her stopping didn't disrupt the music.

Adriana stared past the cameras that were recording the performance. Yes, it was definitely Joao Ramires. His hair was cut different. Back home he'd worn it long, but now it was short; he also sported a beard and mustache that he'd not previously had. But Adriana had no doubt that he was the one; particularly not once he'd bent his head sideways in that specific and unmistakable gesture he had, while indicating to his date that they proceed to the bar, where as usual, Maggie was holding the fort while Eddie performed on stage.

Joao's date was a thirtyish Caucasian blonde; pretty but weathered.

Oddly enough though, Joao showed no sign of having recognized Adriana. She found this strange, how, other than for a single glance at the stage, and a disinterested one at that, he paid no attention to her.

What's he doing here? she asked herself. *And if I can recognize him so easily, how is it that he no longer recognizes me?*

Joao and his date were now seated at a table. The girl was chatting excitedly to him; while he looked blasé and bored, almost as if he was on drugs. Though he nodded his head while drinking his beer, he still paid little attention to the performance on stage. When he did look their way, his eyes fixed on Eddie, who was giving a good demonstration of how to pound on tom toms, and not on Adriana.

Adriana tried to remember whether or not the sign outside the club that announced Rory's concert had her name anywhere on it. Or maybe Joao had found out about her through the internet? She couldn't ponder long on this though, because Rory was already looking at her and nodding, indicating that he wanted them both to rejoin Eddie once this sequence of snare drum rolls was over. Apparently, Rory had been looking at her for some time now, trying to get her attention without letting the crowd realize she was daydreaming.

Adriana nodded and they hit it together on the beat. The crowd howled and cheered; the music took over again, and Adriana forgot about Joao Ramires for a time.

When next they had a break and she could focus off the music again, Joao Ramires was gone. She'd have thought that maybe he'd just gone to use the men's room, but his date had left too.

Adriana heaved a sigh of relief. At least she didn't have to deal with this tonight.

***

"Hey, what happened to you back then?" Rory asked after the concert. "Ya looked worse than if you'd seen a ghost."

Adriana forced a laugh. "Maybe I did see a ghost, man. I'm not too sure myself."

Rory laughed his jovial laugh and walked off to the bar to get another beer. In a few minutes, tonight's elderly bar patrons were slapping him on the back and telling him how listening to him tonight had brought back sweet memories of the good old days when they were all stoned youngsters. One old guy, even older than Rory, admitted to playing Rory's recording of *What a Wonderful World* at his wedding.

Adriana walked off to the ladies' room. Finding herself alone in there, she stared at her reflection in the washstand mirror. She gripped the edge of the washstand and ruminated on what had happened.

No, I'm not mistaken. I'd be willing to swear under oath that that was Joao I saw during our performance.

However, certainty that it was him brought with it complications.

What the hell does Joao want here? Is he looking for me? And if he is, what does he want with me? I remember that mama said he'd threatened to get me, but does he still wants to hurt me? I'm no threat to him. I didn't even know he was here in Wheeling.

The questions merely agitated her further. After a while, she heard the restroom door open. Two elderly women walked in.

"Hey, you were great tonight," one of them complimented Adriana.

"Thanks," Adriana replied, running the tap and washing her hands.

"Yeah, I wish I could play like that," the other lady said, and then she began whistling one of the tunes Rory had played. "My late husband Joe always loved that song. He used to play it so much it drove me crazy, but now that he's gone, I find that it's one of my most cherished memories of him and of our time together."

"That's so touching," Adriana said.

She left the two women in the ladies' room and returned to the bar. Her first thought was to discuss the matter of Joao's reappearance with Maggie. But Maggie was busy with Eddie at the bar, laughing along with Rory.

Well, Joao's already left, so at the moment there's no problem, Adriana decided. *I'm just scared that he might return. I'll discuss the matter with Maggie tomorrow. She'll be able to advise me on whether or not to inform the police.*

CHAPTER 34

Tom stared at the gun on the coffee table, a Taurus Millennium 9mm, and shook his head. *It's not gotten that bad yet. Yes, my eyesight has really degenerated in the past three weeks, but not to the point where I'm gonna stick a gun in my mouth.*

He'd purchased the gun years ago, when he and Maggie had lived in a less secure area of town where the residents were plagued with constant break-ins. Thankfully, he'd never had to use the weapon. That had been a relief to both he and Maggie; not having to stand over the bullet-riddled body of some misguided kid who thought burglary was the way to the high life.

Since moving to this pleasant neighborhood on Quail Court, however, the gun had lain in a hatbox, forgotten for years. It was only recently, when considering how much time Maggie spent down at the club now things were moving again, that it had occurred to Tom that she might need protection. Not from club patrons, but rather, on those nights when for whatever reason, exercise or what-have-you, Maggie might decide to walk home, rather than drive. Even though the club was barely a mile from their home, a mile could prove a very long distance to walk alone at night. Even in a quiet neighborhood like this there were potential predators ready to take advantage of a helpless woman once alcohol had overridden their natural abhorrence to committing crime.

So, Tom had unearthed the gun and left it in the middle drawer of Maggie's nightstand. She had however tacitly refused to take it with her when leaving the house. Tom hadn't complained; he figured that sooner or later she would either hear about or read something in the news that would change her mind.

It was only tonight that Tom had thought of the gun as a way out for himself.

But no, not yet. I'm not suffering yet and killing myself when I'm in no pain at all would be a cowardly thing to do. Not to mention that I'd be leaving Maggie all alone by herself. He grimaced. *But that's the thing, isn't it? Maggie doesn't seem to see anything wrong with leaving me here by myself!*

For a few moments this injustice enraged him. He calmed himself, and immediately understood that irrational bursts of bad temper like this were the primary reason his wife was staying away from him as much as she could. His irrational anger, his continually verbally lashing out at Maggie because there was no one else to take out his frustrations on, was driving a wedge between them and ruining his marriage.

Depression filled his soul. *No, I'm not much of a husband at the moment. I mustn't make Maggie suffer. God knows, she already carrying enough of a burden, just thinking of what's to come for both of us, without me adding more to it.*

He picked up the other object on the coffee table, a Bible. The Bible had turned up in the house when either Maggie or Adriana had gotten it in their heads that they go to church. Tom wasn't sure whose idea it had been, but for two Sundays in a row, both women had visited the Bethlehem Apostolic Temple, the small church just a short drive from the *Jazzy Truth*. Tom felt that sooner or later, Maggie and Adriana would both just as quickly lost their religious fervor, but the Bible had come from those visits.

Tom flipped the black book open and attempted reading it, then immediately quit in frustration. He could barely make out the print, each line of text was merely a thick black bar, the two rows of text per page looking like descending sets of eyebrows.

Disgusted, Tom threw the Bible across the room, then immediately regretted doing so. He got up and crossed the living room and retrieved the Bible. He replaced the Bible on the coffee table, and then picked up the gun to return it to Maggie's nightstand drawer before she returned home.

The gun itself was just a metallic and molded polymer blur, its outlines undefined except in Tom's memory. Likewise, the living room in which he sat retained its shape more in his mind that in the images his eyes currently fed him. He still had times when the world was a normal place, but the periods of blurriness were longer-lasting now. Tom refrained from mentioning most of the episodes to Maggie; he didn't wish to scare her. What was happening to him was inevitable, his wife's fright and worry would simply complicate matters further, by upsetting and not helping her.

While putting the gun away, Tom was hit by a fresh burst of depression. The feeling of blackness swept over him with such fury that he almost said, "To hell with it all!" pulled the gun out and got it over with.

But instead, he firmly shut the drawer, lay in bed, and filled his mind with pleasant thoughts of Maggie.

He felt impatient for her return from the club, so he could tell her how much he loved her and apologize for how badly he'd been treating her of recent.

Tomorrow will be a better day for both of us, for sure, he told himself wistfully, and with the sincere intention to change his grouchy behavior for the better. *Whatever time I've got left, I intend to share it with Maggie in love and happiness. Then, when I depart this life, it won't be with regret for how badly I've treated her.*

CHAPTER 35

It was almost 1 a.m. before the last club patrons left for home.

Old Rory Davis had gone to bed in Eddie's apartment.

Assisted by his girlfriend Traci, Eddie was doing some last-minute tidying up.

At the rear of the club, Adriana was walking Maggie over to her car.

"Oh, tonight was great," Maggie said as she unlocked the SUV from her keyring. "You guys were really cookin'."

"Yeah, Rory really brought out the best in both Eddie and myself," Adriana admitted.

Maggie beamed at her and then hugged her. "Oh, don't be so modest. Without you, none of it would have worked. Eddie's reliable, but you're the glue holding it all together now." She stepped back from Adriana and gestured at the club building. "If you hadn't agreed to come work here, I'd most likely be out of business for good now."

Adriana giggled. "Oh, it can't have been *that* bad." She was glad to see Maggie happy. Yes, Maggie had had a few drinks tonight, but her happiness wasn't merely coming from her alcohol consumption. Adriana sensed a real change in her, evidenced by a genuine, rekindled desire to see Tom. It was evident in Maggie's eyes that beginning from tonight, things would be very different for the couple.

Seeing how happy Maggie was had already decided Adriana to not discuss the Joao Ramires case until tomorrow afternoon.

"Okay, goodnight, girl. Time to get back to my Tom," Maggie said.

Then, just as Maggie was about to pull the car door open, Adriana sensed movement from the corner of her eyes. She leapt aside, just in time to avoid a knife slash.

She turned and saw Joao Ramires standing there.

"What do you want?" she asked in fear. "I knew it was you earlier in the club."

"Who the hell are you?" Maggie asked, her fear dampened somewhat by her alcohol consumption. "What do you want with Adriana?"

Joao held the knife out towards them, its blade glinting nastily in the moonlight. His posture was slightly unsteady; his eyes a little glazed.

"I'm the one who shot Adriana's brother and now I'm here to kill her too," he brashly declared to Maggie.

"Why kill me, Joao?" Adriana asked, totally confused by this turn of events.

"So, you don't give me away to the police!" Joao growled back at her.

He lunged at Adriana, but again she escaped him.

Maggie meanwhile lunged at Joao, yelling, "Leave her alone, you bastard!"

Joao froze for a moment and then his face turned into a mask of rage, and he stabbed Maggie in the belly. He pulled away his hand; it was covered with blood. However, Maggie was still holding onto him, so Joao stabbed her again.

"Noooo!" Adriana screamed as Maggie slumped to the floor, the front of her blue tee shirt awash with red. "Stop it, you idiot. What are you doing!?"

But Joao was already turning toward Adriana. The crazed look on his face spoke of him being on drugs. He lunged at Adriana again and this time caught her, cutting her along her right forearm.

"Now I will kill you too, woman. And your lips will be sealed forever!"

Joao advanced on Adriana, who backed away from him. She was torn between bending to help Maggie, who was jerking on the floor and spitting blood from her lips, and fleeing to save herself.

"Hey, what the hell's going on over there!?" Eddie's voice rang out from the back door of the club.

"Help!" Adriana screamed. "He's hurt Maggie!"

Eddie threw down the bag of trash he'd brought out to dispose of and ran towards them.

Joao took a few seconds to size up the approaching man, and then ran off into the surrounding trees.

Eddie reached Adriana and started to run past her in pursuit of the intruder, but one look down at Maggie stopped him. Maggie was coughing up blood by the second. Her eyes were already shut, and her chest rose and fell rapidly.

"Call an ambulance!" he told Adriana. "Call an ambulance now!"

Eddie squatted beside Maggie and tried to wake her up.

Functioning on complete autopilot because of her disbelief of the current situation, Adriana got out her cellphone and dialed 911. She told the emergency operator what had happened, gave the man the club's address, and hung up.

When she looked at Eddie again, she saw that his eyes were filled with tears.

She looked down at Maggie. Maggie lay limp on the ground with blood continuing to pool around her. Adriana knew the ambulance she'd just called for would arrive way too late. Margaret Duchensky was already dead.

Adriana dropped to her knees beside Eddie, gripped Maggie's rapidly cooling hand, and began weeping copiously too.

CHAPTER 36

Tom sat at the front of the funeral parlor, with his older sister Sharon on his right hand and Adriana on his left.

One week later, Maggie's death still made no sense to Tom. Of course, there was nothing cryptic about her passing; she'd been killed by an old acquaintance of Adriana's, the same hoodlum who had shot and paralyzed Adriana's brother back in Brazil.

The killer—Joao Ramires—was still at large. The police thought he'd fled the state, but they weren't sure.

***

As for *how* Joao had found Adriana again? That had to be the most ironic coincidence of all time. It turned out that Joao's father Manuel Ramires had once played bongos with Rory Davis during one of Rory's Brazilian tours back in the 90s. Joao had grown up hearing his father tell of the great times he and Rory had had on the road together, and so when his American girlfriend Corrine discovered Rory would be playing at the Jazzy Truth, Joao had decided to check him out, and had driven over from Cleveland, Ohio to catch the gig.

Corrine Phillips had come forward herself once the crime hit the news and this was the story she had told the police.

Even odder, Joao hadn't recognized Adriana at all. He'd noticed that the jazz trio's keyboard player seemed to be checking him out, and had joked to Corrine that he thought she was interested in him. It was only when one of the old-timers at the bar had asked Maggie who the fantastic female piano player was that Joao realized she was Mario Fernandez's older sister. This then spelt trouble for Adriana, because (according to Corrine), Joao now realized that she'd recognized him when he'd walked into the club. He'd told Corrine that Adriana was sure to 'rat him out to the cops,' and that he needed to have a private talk with her to convince her not to do so. The nature of that 'private talk' was now headline news, though Corrine claimed that all Joao had told her when he'd left their motel room later that night to return to the club, was that he intended to threaten Adriana, nothing more.

Corrine also said she'd not seen Joao since he left the motel. He'd neither returned to their motel room that night, nor contacted her since then.

While the police believed her story that Joao's encountering Adriana again was completely accidental, they doubted that Maggie's killer hadn't contacted her since then. However, phone records partially confirmed her story.

***

"Margaret Duchensky was a well-known local figure," the minister officiating her funeral said. "She was a vibrant woman, one who helped unify our little community and spread joy through her little jazz club, the Jazzy Truth. I'll share a secret with you all—I visited her jazz club myself a few times. Mind you, only to listen to the wonderful music, not to get drunk."

After a little polite laughter, he went on: "But, folks, my point here is, that the measure of a person's life isn't how *long* one lives for, but how *well* one lives during that period. And by 'how well' I'm referring to how much of a positive impact the departed had on others while they were alive. And I'm certain all of us gathered here to pay our last respects to our departed sister Margaret Duchensky will agree with me that she had a good and positive impact on our lives, an impact that I suspect will extend far beyond her grave . . . ."

Sharon smiled and squeezed Tom's hand. He smiled back, although he could hardly see her face. It seemed to him that Maggie's death had accelerated the decline of his eyesight. Yes, he still had long stretches of clear vision, but unfortunately, this time of the funeral wasn't one of them. He had pills for the accompanying headaches, but nothing could help his eyes.

He'd already explained to his sister that he had been 'having some trouble with his eyes.'

He glanced left, towards Adriana, who was currently as blurry as figure to him as everyone else in the funeral hall.

Try as much as he might, he couldn't fault her at all in this. True, she and not Maggie had actually been the murderer's target, but she wasn't to blame here. In the immediate aftermath of his wife's murder, Tom had thought long and hard about this. He'd needed a target for his boiling rage, and he'd sought that target in Maggie's Brazilian protégé. But he'd found trying to pin the blame on Adriana to be an exercise in futility; his conscience was the brick wall that consistently exonerated her of guilt.

So now he smiled at her too, suddenly aware that her tears had ruined her makeup. Just as his older sister had just done to him, he sought her right hand and squeezed it comfortingly, taking care not to brush against her stitched forearm. She squeezed his hand back reassuringly, and Tom was struck by the fact that this was the first instance of any physical contact between them.

The minister spoke on, more words about Margaret's sterling character which Tom completely approved of. Then Adriana left Tom's side and joined Eddie, Rory Davis and Tolbert Hawes for a rousing jazz performance of *It Is Well with My Soul* that left most of the audience in tears.

***

If it was possible for one to nurse a bigger regret than being abruptly separated from the person one loved, Tom felt it. At the moment, his biggest regret was that now, he would never be able to follow through with his resolution to treat Maggie better than he'd been doing. In fact, his guilty memory of how badly he'd behaved towards Maggie in the weeks before her death was a major factor in his exonerating Adriana from any perceived guilt with regards to Maggie's death.

As to how Tom felt after Maggie's passing? 'Shipwrecked' would be an accurate description. He mentally likened himself to a thirsty man who discovered that what was supposedly the last bottle of water on Earth actually contained gasoline or bleach.

***

Maggie's casket passed through the damask curtain at the rear of the hall, en route to the incinerator, and her funeral ended.

Shepherded by Sharon, Tom greeted the funeral attendees. These were many and varied, lots of them musicians who'd worked with Maggie over the years. The one glaring absentee among the mourners was Jerry Bennet, the Jazzy Truth's resident pianist before Adriana. But Jerry's absence could be easily explained: the young man was on tour in Poland, and not being particularly consistent with his social media, hadn't learnt about Maggie's death until the day before yesterday.

Other than for Jerry, most of Maggie's extended musical family was represented. And with this in mind, the funeral reception was held at the Jazzy Truth jazz club, culminating in an extended jam session that lasted till the early hours of the next morning.

During the jam session, Tom felt a kaleidoscope of emotions. His vision had returned for a while and so he had no need to be shepherded from place to place by his sister. He sat up close to the stage and let the music wash over him.

For the first time in his life, it hurt him that he wasn't musical; that he never would be able to appreciate music the way Maggie had. Loving music to the same degree that she had—and deriving that similar enjoyment from her favorite records after her death—would have been a connection between them now, something to cherish and hold on to.

Tom sat in place through the whole jam session, getting a little drunk with the musicians, but mostly nursing his pain and trying not to freefall into depression.

Maggie's death was so needless, he thought as the hours rolled past. *If Death wanted to kill someone, why not just take me, who's already halfway there? I'd have gladly gone in her place.*

It was only after the jam session concluded with the dawn, that everyone, Tom included, agreed that Maggie Duchensky had been properly laid to rest.

As Tom later told both his sister and Adriana: "Given the chance, this is exactly how Maggie would have planned her funeral."

PART FIVE:
THE BLIND MELODY

CHAPTER 37

A week after the funeral, Adriana still couldn't remember Maggie without her eyes filling with tears.

"Her death still hurts me so bad, mama," she told her mother during a video call on the Thursday after the funeral service. "Losing her is one of the worst things that's ever happened to me."

Her mother's miniature image nodded sagely. The old woman was sad too that her daughter's best friend had died. "Does this mean you'll be coming back home to Brazil then?" she asked in Portuguese.

Adriana shook her head. Today, speaking her native tongue with her mother didn't hold the comfort it usually did. "Oh, mama, I don't know yet. At the moment, everything here is so confusing. The club has been shut since Maggie's death. Eddie and I don't know what is going to happen to it."

"How is Mr. Duchensky doing?"

"Not very good. He seems to be falling apart. His older sister stayed in town after the wake to be with him these past two weeks, but she lives in Indiana—that's another American state, mama; in fact, it's two states away from here—and she needs to get back to her life and her own family. So, we don't know what's going to happen here. I might be out of a job in a few days—in fact, I may already be out of a job."

"I'm sure it'll all work out for the best, dear. You can always go back to the cruise ship."

Adriana nodded. "I hope it won't come to that. I'd like to keep working here in America. I like it here. I like this town; these people. I love this jazz club, and I'd like to see it succeed."

"Yesterday, you said Mr. Duchensky wants to see you about the club. Has he said when?"

"Yes, mama. He said he'll be here this afternoon." Adriana checked the time on her watch. "I'm expecting him here in about an hour."

Her mother's little image pixelated a little and then cleared up. The old woman now looked a little perplexed. "But . . . but, dear, you said he can't see very well anymore. Wouldn't it make more sense for you to go and see him at home?"

Adriana nodded. "I suggested that to him, mama, but he said he'd prefer our discussion to happen here, where his wife used to work."

"Yes, that makes sense, but still—"

"Oh, mama, I really don't want to come back to Brazil yet! But from what Mr. Duchensky hinted, we're going to be discussing exactly that: either how to keep the club running, or to shut it down and . . . he mentioned his paying my fare home if I want to leave the USA."

"He sounds like a very nice man."

"He is, mama. It's just that—"

Adriana's mother interrupted her with a worried look on her face: "Adriana, have the American police arrested that crazy Joao Ramires yet?"

Adriana's own look of worry replied her mother before her voice did. "They haven't, mama. That's my biggest worry now. The police have already advised me to move from here. According to them Joao might come back here to kill me because I'm the only actual witness to Maggie's murder. Eddie didn't get a clear look at him that night, but I did."

"Oh my God, that is terrible. But where can you move to?"

"That's the problem. At the moment, I can't afford to move anywhere else. I'm running out of money as it is, and if you remember, this apartment is rent free, part of my employment package. It meant Maggie could pay me less money than I'd earn elsewhere and I'd still be comfortable."

Her mother's facial expression became extremely agitated. "But you have to leave the place! What if Joao does come back to kill you?"

Adriana sighed and replied, "I really hope he doesn't come back here, mama. Because, right now, I've nowhere else to go."

CHAPTER 38

Tom took an Uber to the club. At the moment, his vision was half-and-half, more blurs and shapes than clear objects, and he didn't want to bother Sharon with driving him.

Sharon was worried about how he'd cope by himself once she left for home in two days' time.

"You don't even have a guide dog yet," she pointed out. "How will you get around?"

"I'll be fine," he replied in what he hoped was a confident voice. "I still see fine most of the time. I'll get a dog and cane when my vision has almost completely failed."

He got out of the Uber and walked to the club. The walk from the vehicle to the front door was a short one, and he couldn't miss his way even if his eyesight failed.

Yes, a short walk, but one laden with memories. He remembered the first time he'd come here with Maggie and met her father also; the old man grimly welcoming, a king realizing that his cherished princess would soon be leaving the family castle. He also remembered helping Maggie redecorate the place after her father's death.

Tears were forming in his eyes when he reached the front door.

The club was open. Eddie was out in town for the day, but before leaving he'd rolled up the metal shutter over the entrance so Tom could get in when he arrived.

Tom pushed the door open and stepped inside; and was immediately assailed by familiar scents and colors. True, he couldn't see the bar or tables or the chairs clearly, but their fuzzy contours assembled in his memory into clear impressions of what was where.

Tom wasn't really concerned about Eddie. Eddie was a bartender. Just like waitresses, bartenders seldom had trouble finding employment. And besides, Eddie was an American citizen; he could travel, live, and work anywhere in the country.

No, Tom's primary concern was Adriana.

Personally, Tom had no drive to keep the club going. Maggie had been an only child and so the entire Jazzy Truth premises legally belonged to him now, but he had no desire to do anything at all with it. His personal inertia seemed to increase by the hour. Even the idea of selling the place didn't interest him. His work retirement package had been substantial, in addition to which he would also be receiving a substantial payment from Maggie's life insurance policy. Combined, the money would be enough to keep him going comfortably for many years to come.

Ironic of course, as he didn't have 'many years' in which to spend his money.

What's the point of working when you're dying? If I wasn't dying myself, I'm sure I'd keep the club going simply to keep Maggie's memory alive in the community, but now, really, what's the damn point of anything at all?

Then he had to laugh, really laugh out loud. *Oh, and don't I believe Sharon knows it too? I've been unable to find Maggie's gun since she arrived at the house. She's most likely hidden it somewhere, or even buried it out back.*

He hadn't bothered asking Sharon what she had done with his gun. Since Maggie's death he no longer felt suicidal. He just felt low, compressed by the pointlessness of human activity as a whole.

I guess I might kill myself if I could find the gun, but I don't even have the drive to fight Sharon for it.

He yawned—a side-effect of the medication the doctors had him on because of his headaches—and made his way over to a couch near the stage. All the way his head filled with memories: friends walking this same floor and taking seats . . . musicians from home and abroad up on the stage, filling the air with happiness . . . Maggie laughing and dancing and kissing him tenderly after everyone had gone home . . .

Sitting on the couch itself brought back even more memories. Back then, before they'd torn out the old-time booths to create more floor space for tables, he'd proposed to Maggie from a couch just like this one. Tom smiled at the recollection of Maggie's shocked surprise when in the midst of dinner with their friends, she'd discovered the diamond ring in her martini.

The smile now left Tom's face and was replaced by a steady stream of tears. *Oh, honey, why'd you have to die so needlessly?*

Now that the tears had begun, they just wouldn't stop. Tom sat there on the couch, crying for the lost past.

He'd left home early and didn't expect Adriana to show up for at least thirty minutes yet. He could call her, but phoning people was a drag now that he couldn't make out the screen phone clearly.

So instead, Tom decided to wait. He sat there on the couch, weeping his heart out and then the headache medicine kicked in and he fell soundly asleep.

CHAPTER 39

When Adriana arrived in the club, she found Tom fast asleep on a couch.

Okay, now this is unexpected.

The slumbering man had a look of misery on his face like he was suffering in his dreams. She considered waking him up, but then changed her mind.

Her conversation with her mother had left her with a heavy heart; a lot of it having to do with the fact that Tom was here right now to spell out what her immediate future would be, that in just a few minutes, an hour at most, she would most likely be receiving her severance pay from him, along with his polite request that she quit the premises.

Adriana suspected he would also sell the club to be free from Maggie's memory.

It's what I'd do in his shoes.

But, she still had the interval before he woke up to enjoy these surroundings again. Of course, she expected that she'd be allowed in here as often as she liked until she moved out of her apartment, but she knew it wouldn't feel the same.

At the moment I'm an integral part of this place, and it is a part of me. Once the connection is severed, once Tom terminates my appointment as the club's resident musician, my relationship to this place becomes completely illusory.

With that grim thought in mind, Adriana walked over to the stage, climbed up on it and sat behind the electric piano. She turned it and its amplifier on, made sure the volume was quite low and began playing.

She soon lost herself in the music and began singing too. Every now and then she looked over at Tom and smiled sadly, in a shared sense of loss with him.

***

Tom woke up and there was music in the air.

In a few seconds he understood that it was Adriana playing the piano and singing. He made an initial effort to get up from the couch, but a deep tiredness was still on him and so he lay back where he was and waited till he felt stronger.

Lying there on his back and with his vision even more cloudy than previously, all he had was the music; Adriana's musical vision in place of the vision of his eyes.

Her voice was soft and uncertain, and she was singing in her native Portuguese, but Tom nonetheless felt the sorrow in her words.

Then she stopped singing and simply played the piano. And possibly for the first time since he and Maggie had first heard Adriana play on the cruise ship, Tom really listened to her playing. Now, without sight to distract him, he heard the inexplicable talent she possessed, that musical magic that had determined his just laid-to-rest wife to take a chance on her. He heard the magic of Adriana's fingers as they traversed the piano keyboard, felt the beauty of the scales she played.

He doubted that Adriana knew he was awake yet and he maintained the illusion of his slumber for the benefit of hearing her play on. At first her playing was as mournful as the song she'd been singing when he awoke. But then, stage by stage it grew brighter, until finally she was playing happiness into his ears. Happiness, the emotion he'd forgotten existed. She played and he smiled and got to his feet.

She immediately ceased playing. "Oh, I'm sorry I woke you," she apologized.

He smiled in her direction. "No, go on playing. I like what I'm hearing. Please turn the music up."

She turned the volume up. The music now filled the club.

Tom had to go to her. He just had to. He felt compelled by the music, drawn by it on invisible strings to the side of the woman making that irresistible melody that now filled him with pleasure. He knew his sadness still lurked around him, but for the moment it was scared, scared off by the beautiful sounds this woman was making. He wanted to stand by her side by the piano and smile down at her, even if he couldn't see her face.

Taking care to avoid the blurred furniture, he stepped away from the couch and headed across the room towards Adriana.

But just as he neared the stage, he felt his foot snag on a cable. He tripped and was unable to right his balance—there was nothing nearby for him to steady himself against—and went flying through the air.

He struck his head against the wall and his blurred world turned completely black.

CHAPTER 40

Tom awoke to a vision of crystal clarity. He was staring up at an angel. A beautiful angel.

He blinked. No, he hadn't killed himself yet. He was back on the couch, lying on his back and with his head cradled in Adriana's lap. She was pressing an icepack to his left temple, which throbbed with a passing headache.

She smiled down at him in relief. "I was wondering whether or not to call for an ambulance."

Suddenly he felt uncomfortable by this close proximity to her and tried to get up.

"Don't," she chided gently. "Just stay exactly how you are till you're sure you feel better."

"Someone might come in," Tom countered, though her kindness and concern touched him immensely. "Who knows what they'll think?"

She laughed gently. "Someone already did. Eddie came in right after you knocked yourself out. He was the one who lifted you back onto the couch. How else would I have gotten you over here? You're too heavy for me to have managed it on my own."

Tom grudgingly accepted defeat. "Where's Eddie now?"

"He's gone out again. Said I was to give him a call if you needed to go to the ER."

Tom relaxed. The club was still closed and other than Eddie, he didn't think anyone else would be coming round today.

Still, it felt awkward to be lying here like this, staring up into the angelic face of another woman. A beautiful woman for that matter, though he'd never allowed himself to consider that aspect of Adriana Fernandez while Maggie was alive.

Nor now that I'm a widower either, he reminded himself. *I don't need more complications in my life. Nor does she.*

"That was a wonderful song you were singing," he said. "What was it?"

"I call it *My Happy Uncertainty.* It's about the future, a perfect future I would love to have with the man I love, but which seems out of reach to me. I wrote it back home in Brazil, before the pandemic."

"I couldn't understand a word you sang, but I felt what you felt."

She smiled down at him and unconsciously stroked his hair. "That is perfect. Many times, feelings are more true than words."

And that was how the conversational ice between them was broken. Without knowing how the distracted flow of words began, Tom found himself chatting with Adriana about a myriad of things. Traveling, love and death, happiness and sadness. Loss and loneliness, supermarkets and pets, comparing life here in the USA and south of the US border. Everything.

They chatted about everything in fact, except the thing Tom had come to the club to discuss, namely Adriana's future. The time passed like a rapidly-flowing river, with the two of them passengers adrift in a boat afloat on it.

At a point, after Tom finally sat up and put the icepack aside, Adriana confessed to him that she knew about his illness. That prompted a burst of weeping on her part which wound up with Tom consoling her as if she was the one dying.

She impressed Tom with her concern for him, despite his never being close to her in the past. The longer they talked, the more Tom realized that he really didn't want to let Adriana go out of his life just yet. Not just because she was a bridge to Maggie—a way to hold on to the cherished past, nor because of her impeccable talent as a musician—but because he was suddenly discovering that he really liked her as a person. She'd made him happy, made him laugh, and it seemed like he was having the same effect on her.

I want to help her, but how? What can I do for her?

After about two hours of talking about everything under the sun, something occurred to him:

"Listen, Adriana, I spoke to the police this morning about Joao. They still have no clue where he is."

Adriana nodded back at him. "I don't know where he could be hiding. I think he might have run back to Brazil. But our police want him too for Renato Barbosa's murder so he may hide in Mexico or Panama instead."

Tom nodded. "But until that's confirmed, what are you going to do? It's dangerous for you to remain here at the club."

She sighed. "I don't know, Tom. I know it's dangerous in case Joao comes looking for me, but I've no money to rent somewhere else to live."

Tom took a deep breath and then took the plunge. "I'm thinking. At the moment I live alone. Why don't you move in with me?"

"What?" Her eyes widened in surprise; it was obvious she'd been expecting anything but this. The strained expression on her face while she'd been answering his queries about the safety of the upstairs apartment had told him she'd thought this was it, he was about to kick her out of the building and send her off home to Belém in Brazil.

"Listen," he went on quickly before she had time to refuse. "my house has loads of space and three bedrooms. If you come over you can have the guestroom at the back. You remember it, don't you? It's the one you lived in when you first got here, while Maggie was having your apartment above the club renovated."

She nodded cautiously. "It's not that I wouldn't like to, but . . . but . . ."

Tom smiled reassuringly. "I'll be honest with you, Adriana. At the moment I don't know what I'm going to do about the club. But you know I'm going blind and I'm dying too. I need someone with me . . . Listen, for the moment at least you can be my P.A., secretary, cook, housekeeper, whatever you want to call it—you'll mostly be functioning as my eyes. I'll pay you the same salary you earned here at the club, plus bonuses."

Again, she nodded cautiously. He could tell that she was pleased by the offer but didn't want to seem too eager.

"Anyway, what do you say to us trying the arrangement out for a month or two. If you think it's not working, you can quit anytime you want. There's two cars if you don't mind taking driving lessons."

He stopped, his heart racing (though if asked, he couldn't have said why), and waited for her response.

Finally, she nodded. "Okay, Tom, I don't mind moving in with you and being your eyes for the meantime. But . . ." she smiled shyly, "but, Tom, what are the neighbors going to think?"

He grinned, glad that she'd accepted his proposal. "The one person whose opinion I'm worried about is my sister Sharon. We'll wait till she's safely on her way back home before I move you in."

CHAPTER 41

It was now three weeks since Adriana had begun living with Tom, and her feelings about their domestic arrangement were mixed.

As she made morning coffee for both of them, her concerns were uppermost in her mind.

Mama wants me to move out but admits there's nowhere better I can go at the moment.

Her mother's concern was a logical one. Back home in Brazil, in her almost-slum neighborhood where everyone lived almost on top of each other, such a living arrangement as she had with Tom now would stink of intense sluttiness on her part.

"Why, Adriana," her mother had pointed out. "His wife's not been dead two months yet!"

"It's okay, mama," she'd carefully explained. "I already told you there's nothing going on between us."

"There had better not be," her mother had replied.

"Don't worry, mama, he's not showing the slightest interest in me."

Her mother had hopefully accepted that lie at face value.

Well, it isn't really a lie, Adriana thought while pouring their steaming coffee into twin mugs. *Tom really isn't showing any interest in me. At least he's doing his best not to show his interest. And myself?*

Yes, and herself? It was hard to put into thoughts because it was a thing of the soul, but whenever Adriana Fernandez permitted herself to think about it, she realized that she too was slowing becoming emotionally involved with Tom Duchensky.

Actually, 'becoming' was the wrong world. Except for the ethical barrier of Tom's wife's recent death, Adriana would have had no problem admitting that she was very much in love with her current housemate.

This was the problem. She liked the way she felt, but both thought that she shouldn't be feeling the way she did, and also felt frustrated that she couldn't express herself freely to Tom.

All my life I've been waiting for the right man and now that my heart is finally hooked on someone, he turns out to be the wrong man, for all kinds of crazy reasons, all of which make perfectly logical sense, but which don't do me any good.

Even more problematic for her was the fact that Tom clearly felt the same way she did. He had never said anything suggesting romance to her, or even hinted that he liked her in such a way; but she was a woman, she could read him like a book now. Tom's unexpressed desire for her simply made things worse because, while unrequited love can be resisted and in time discarded, restrained love is a totally different beast, a creature certain to burst loose at the most awkward of times.

Adriana picked up both mugs of coffee and returned to the breakfast table with them.

Eddie's suggestion is the best one: work for a few more months till I've earned enough cash to rent a place of my own, and then move out of here. I can still work as Tom's eyes, but I won't have to worry about wagging tongues. So, I think that is exactly what I'm going to do. Oh, but that doesn't really help my state of heart, does it?

She reached the breakfast table and laughed while setting down the cups. "Sorry about this; I'm still not used to preparing breakfast in an ordinary fashion. Most mornings I used to simply grab a sandwich while dashing out of the house."

Tom smiled back at her. Today was one of those day when he could hardly see. It hurt her, but it also helped her cope with her own feelings to realize that he couldn't read the longing in her eyes.

***

Tom smiled as he ate his breakfast. By now he was getting used to feeling his way around the house, and not being able to see his plate didn't bother him as much as being unable to read the words on his laptop screen once had.

It's a process. Life in reverse. I'm a clock spring winding down to midnight.

The thing was, with Adriana living here and looking after him, Tom felt happy; that same happiness that he'd felt that afternoon two weeks ago on which he'd made what he liked to think of as his 'proposal' to her.

The same joy he'd experienced then filled him again each time he heard her voice.

He knew he'd fallen in love with her that afternoon. But oh, such a love was forbidden. It must be. He had loved Maggie wholeheartedly, had never cheated on her, nor ever wanted to; and so, knowing that that had been the case, he now wondered how he could have for Adriana equally strong feelings of a similar kind.

No, no, no. It can't be right. I'm merely on the rebound. It's a good thing she has no idea of my feelings for her. It would result in ridicule.

And yet, on those days where his optical darkness lightened for a few hours and he saw her face clearly, there seemed to him to be no mistaking the emotions he read in her eyes. It seemed impossible to him that she could share his feelings for her.

He chewed a strip of bacon, listened to the sound of Adriana crunching toast between her teeth and tried not to let her see that he was moping.

I know she's a good, clean-hearted soul. I know she's taking care of me because she wants to, not because she's seeking to gain anything from doing so. I'm a hundred percent certain that Adriana has no ulterior motives in this. Okay, yes, maybe she feels a sense of obligation to look after me because she was Maggie's friend and protégé, but I can hardly imagine—hardly dare hope—that she's being so nice to me because she loves me.

He saddened. *What's there to love anyway? An elderly and sick man who'll soon be underground? A prospective funeral?*

The day before Sharon's departure for home, he and she had scattered Maggie's ashes over the Ohio River. Is that what he too would leave behind for Adriana if he professed his love for her and—the impossible—she accepted him?

No, I couldn't do that to her. Never in a million years.

So instead, he smiled in Adriana's general direction, and asked: "Are you still going to pick up your tablet device from the club this evening?"

He thrilled to the sound of her voice when she replied. "Yeah, I have to. My laptop is completely fried. I'll make do with the tablet till I can afford another one."

Tom laughed. "Addy, I used to work in IT—there are four working laptops in the house; five, if you consider Maggie's. You can use any one of them you like; two or three even if you've that many fingers."

'Addy' was his pet name for her, she seemed to like it.

She laughed. "Okay, if you insist. But I still need to pick up the tablet anyway. There are some music score PDFs that I'll want to transfer to the laptop."

"Okay, that's fine. Should I come with you?"

"No need. I'll just walk there and back after lunch."

"And then you'll play something on the piano for me?" he asked like a child begging his mother for a cookie.

(With the club currently dysfunctional, Adriana had moved the Fender Rhodes electric piano and amplifier over here to the house and set them up in a corner of the living room.)

He sensed her smiling and nodding at him. "Of course. I'll be back as quick as I can, and then I'll play you something from the manuscripts on the tablet."

Tom finished his breakfast with a sense of forbidden delight; the renewed sense that his current happiness was a bad thing.

CHAPTER 42

Adriana arrived at the Jazzy Truth at about 5 p.m.

The rollaway metal shutter over the front door was down, the indication that the club was still closed to business. She stood staring at it for a while.

She and Tom were set to discuss the club's fate tomorrow. He'd had an offer from a prospective buyer and wasn't sure whether or not to sell. Because the lot was so close to the freeway, the buyer wanted to demolish the Jazzy Truth and construct a supermarket in its place.

Adriana intended to convince Tom not to sell the club. It seemed sacrilegious to her that a musical 'temple' should be 'desecrated' solely due to financial interests.

The front lot was empty of cars. Walking around to the rear of the building, she saw that Eddie's hatchback was missing too, meaning he was out, possibly working as bartender at another club.

About to climb the stairs, Adriana paused and quickly looked around the parking lot for intruders. And then, remembering how Joao Ramires had seemed to emerge from nowhere on the night he'd murdered Maggie, she carefully scanned the surrounding trees and bushes for any sign of movement.

Only when she'd decided that the coast was clear did she begin to climb the steps to her apartment. She walked past Eddie's apartment and unlocked her front door.

***

Except for one detail, the interior of Adriana's apartment was exactly the same as she'd left it the last time she'd been here.

That detail was a baseball cap lying on the coffee table.

Adriana at first felt very frightened by the baseball cap, as it wasn't hers. But then she relaxed, realizing that Eddie must have forgotten it in her living room when he'd help her move her things to Tom's house.

Sighing with relief, Adriana walked into her bedroom and found herself face-to-face with Joao Ramires.

Joao was sitting on her bed in his shorts and was pointing a gun at her.

"One squeak out of you and you're history," Joao said in Portuguese, gesturing to her with the gun to come closer to him.

Adriana was so shocked to see Maggie's murderer that her surprise temporarily conquered her fear. "What are you doing in my apartment?" she asked Joao, also speaking their mother tongue, as he got off the bed and stepped up close to her.

He smirked. "What do you think, girl? I've been living here."

Adriana gasped.

Joao tapped his forehead with a finger and went on. "I'm a smart cookie, see? The gringo police will never catch me. I'm always three, four steps ahead of them." He laughed. "I came here one night to ask you why you gave my name to the pigs, and maybe thank you by slitting your throat and giving you a Colombian necktie, and I find that you're not living here no more. So, then I realize this is the one place where the pigs will never check for me, and I move in here."

"But . . . *Eddie?* Eddie lives right next door!" Joao's explanation was so crazy that Adriana thought she must be dreaming.

Joao laughed loudly. "Your friend Eddie has no idea that I'm here. I always leave quietly in the night when he's asleep and I always return before he wakes up; or if I'm late I hide in the bushes until he goes out and then sneak myself in here unseen. Besides, he and his dirty puta of a girlfriend both drink too much. Even if I'm killing someone in here, I doubt that they'll wake up." Joao picked up a tie from the bed and gestured with the gun at Adriana to turn around. "And besides, I always leave the lights off. I'm not foolish, like American gangsters are."

Adriana scowled while Joao first bound her wrists together and then gagged her with a napkin.

"What do you want with me?" she asked before he silenced her.

"Money," he replied. "My funds are low and I need to get out of here; I want to leave this state and head south to Mexico and from there take a boat to Cuba. I threw away my phone, so I can't call Corrine to bring me some cash. She'll be too scared of the pigs to come here anyway. I know my brother Ricardo would give me the money I need, but the police are certain to be on him like glue also."

Joao bound Adriana's ankles together and then shoved her down to the floor and sat on the edge of the bed facing her. This was when she first noticed that his eyes were glazed again, like on the night that he'd stabbed Maggie.

She began sweating profusely.

Oh, my dear God. I should have let Tom walk me here! I shouldn't have come here alone. But how was I supposed to know that this crazy man was in here, that he's been living in my apartment all this while?

"I'm not sure I'll kill you," Joao said. "Do you have any money in this apartment?"

Adriana shook her head.

Joao nodded. "Do you have money in the bank? Your ATM? Hey, woman, don't you dare lie to me. I find out you're lying, and I cut out your tongue!"

Adriana nodded. Yes, she had about a thousand dollars in the bank; the money she was saving up for her new place.

"Good," Joao said. "Now, one more question: Do you have your bank cards with you here?"

Adriana nodded quickly. Her bank cards were in her purse. She saw Joao Ramires visibly relax.

"Good," he said, his voice a low Portuguese growl. "That keeps you alive for now." He walked quickly over to the bedroom window, parted the drapes slightly, and peeked nervously outside. "Okay, so this is what we'll do. For now, we play the waiting game. Once it is dark, you and I will leave the house and go to an ATM, where you will withdraw the money for me. You'll withdraw as much cash as the ATM will pay you. I would have asked you to transfer the money to my bank account, but the police are watching it to locate me. Do you understand?"

Adriana nodded.

"Good. Now be a good girl and sit there patiently until night falls. Do as you're told, and no harm will befall you." Joao got up and peeked out of the window again, and then returned to the bed and lay there staring at the ceiling.

Almost frightened out of her wits now, Adriana stared at her captor and began weeping. She couldn't believe this was happening to her; not after all that she'd already been through.

CHAPTER 43

Adriana had no idea how long she'd been sitting on the floor bemoaning her fate, before she heard knocking on the apartment door.

Before the knocking began, she'd thought Joao was asleep and had toyed with the idea of trying to get to her feet and making a run for it. But she discovered she'd been very mistaken. The moment the knocking began Joao leapt up from the bed as if he'd been fired from a catapult.

"Who the hell is that?" he grumbled in Portuguese, and then rushed to the window and peeked out.

"Dammit. I can't see anyone from here." He left the window and hurried to the living room.

"Hey, Adriana, are you in there?"

Adriana felt her soul flood with desperate hope. It was Tom out there.

"Hey, Adriana, answer me. Are you okay in there?"

She maneuvered sideways from her sitting position and peered down the short corridor that connected to her living room. Joao was kneeling on the armchair by the window, peeking out through barely parted drapes. She watched him leave the window and head back towards her.

"There's a man outside wearing sunglasses, but I don't recognize him."

Tom was still pounding on the apartment door and calling for her. Meanwhile, Joao had picked up his gun from the bed. He reached down and hauled Adriana up to her feet and then after gesturing threatening at her with the gun and putting a finger to his lips, he reached behind her and slipped off the gag.

"Hey, Addy, please answer me if you're in there! You forgot your phone at home, so I couldn't call you to be sure you're okay."

"Who the hell is that idiot?" Joao asked.

"The man who owns this house," Adriana spat at him acidly, though she kept her voice lowered. "The man whose wife you killed. And don't you dare call him an idiot. You're the idiot here. All you do is hurt innocent people. What did Maggie ever do to you, huh?"

"She attacked me, and I panicked, okay? I was a bit high, and it was the heat of the moment!" he whispered in an agitated voice. But now he calmed himself. "Now, listen to me. You are going to open the door and pretend that everything is okay in here. Tell him to go away."

"He won't go away. I'm living with him now."

Joao's eyes widened. "You're sleeping with him? So soon after his wife's death? That is just so damn wrong. I never figured you for a whore."

Adriana grimaced. "No, I'm not sleeping with him, Joao. But he's protecting me. He won't leave without me coming along."

Joao thought on this, then said, "Okay, so invite him in."

"What are you going to do to Tom?"

"Nothing, so long as you do as I say. I didn't plan to kill his wife, and I can't leave too many corpses behind me anyway. Too much heat. I'll just knock him out and we'll leave to get the money. I'll cover my nose and mouth with a scarf so he can't identify me."

Adriana nodded. "And afterwards? What are you going to do with me?"

He frowned back. "Wait and see."

Adriana cringed at the noncommittal reply. She doubted that she would survive this night. But so long as he didn't hurt Tom too, that was okay with her.

Tom's voice came again: "Hey, Adriana, I know you're in there! Open up! I'm becoming worried!"

I'll never forgive myself if Tom dies because of me. I'm the reason he's lost his wife. But no more . . .

"Alright," she told Joao, "I'll lure him in here. But if you dare hurt him, I'll scream my lungs out; doesn't matter if you slit my throat wide open immediately afterwards. You hurt one hair on Tom's head and I'll scream so loud in here that Mr. President will hear me in Washington DC." He frowned at her and she smiled coldly back. "Just remember, Joao, I'm your passport out of here. Don't shoot yourself in the foot."

Joao scowled. "Just open the damn door before he starts getting suspicious."

"Untie me."

Joao quickly wrapped a red scarf around his mouth and nose. Then he untied Adriana and she hurried to the front door with Joao's gun poking her in the back. They reached the door and he stood out of sight, while she unlocked it.

For a moment Adriana considered running outside and pulling Tom after her, but if she did so, it would be too easy for Joao to shoot them both in the back and afterwards hightail it off into the nearby woods again before the cops arrived.

"Adriana, Adriana, open up!"

So I go along with the plan, she thought and pulled the door open.

She forced a smile and stepped back. "Sorry, Tom, I fell asleep. I didn't mean to alarm you. Come inside—"

Tom stepped into the room and hugged her. Adriana now expected Joao to shut the door behind them both, but that wasn't what happened. As Joao moved to shut the door, another man, this one dressed in body armor and holding a light machine gun, kicked the door fully open and dashed into the room. Behind him came another man.

"Police!" Joao grunted and fired at the newcomers.

There was a loud racket of gunfire in the apartment. Adriana closed her eyes and gripped Tom tightly. She was conscious that Tom was pulling her further out of the way and then down to the floor, but she didn't open her eyes until the gunfire ceased.

When she did open her eyes and they both got up again, Joao Ramires lay on the floor in the corridor with blood pouring out of him from what seemed like a hundred holes, while beside him one of the armor-plated policemen was calling for a 'meat wagon' on his walkie-talkie.

Adriana turned away from the horrible sight and gripped Tom again. She was so glad he was safe; so glad that they were both safe.

Adriana had no idea who initiated it or when it began, but she suddenly realized that she was kissing Tom, or he was kissing her, as they stood entwined in the gun smoke-filled apartment.

When, however, she realized what was going on, she gripped Tom tighter and kissed him harder, vowing then that she would never let him go, no matter what happened now.

CHAPTER 44

The lead SWAT officer patiently waited for some of the immediate chaos to calm before approaching the couple. At the moment, an EMT was loading the body of Joao Ramires on to a stretcher.

Although Adriana was elated to be rescued, she was visibly shaken. Even though she'd now stopped kissing Tom, she still clutched him tightly to her; as tightly as she could.

Once the gurney was carted off, the SWAT officer approached the couple.

Adriana looked at the man with many questions in her eyes.

He kept his communication brief, but spoke directly to her: "Mr. Duchensky became worried when he realized you'd left your cellphone at home and hadn't returned from the club an hour and a half later."

Tom shook his head in agreement.

Adriana's heart overflowed with love at the foresight and protective measures he had taken that had ultimately saved her.

The officer continued, nodding at Tom: "So, he called us. Coincidentally, Ms. Miller, the old woman who lives next door to you, called us this morning to complain that for the past three days a Latino-looking man had been trespassing on her property; walking through it in the late hours of the night, and also in the early hours of the morning. So, once we got Mr. Duchensky's phone call also, we put two and two together and decided to investigate . . ."

He talked some more, but Adriana was zoning out from the shock of it all and possibly missed part of what he was saying.

At some point the officer handed Tom a card and mentioned about a trauma team that the FBI had that would be in touch to provide psychological services; and that a detective would be following up with a debrief, etc., but all Adriana wanted to do was hold Tom tight and get the hell out of that apartment.

CHAPTER 45

"I'm so glad all the killing is finally over," Adriana told Tom once they were alone at home again. "I'm also glad that our feelings for one another are out in the open too. I don't know about you, but I've felt close to bursting from not being able to tell you that I love you."

"I'm glad too, honey," Tom said, pulling her closer to him on the living room couch. "But what happens now? We both know the situation here. I'm slowly dying. I love you with all my heart and soul, but, darling, we don't have much time together. It's almost not worth it, for you at least, investing your heart in a living corpse."

He smiled sadly. He'd been unable to see her face when she'd opened the apartment door at the club house, but now he could, and it cheered him up greatly.

Back then he'd kissed her purely on an impulse. He had simply been relieved that she was safe. But his joy had known no bounds when she'd kissed him back, and passionately at that. The touch of her soft lips had filled his soul with unprecedented rapturous delight.

She smiled sadly at him. "I know you're dying, Tom, but I really don't think it matters anymore between us. What matters now is both of us making the most of the time you've got left. Let's think of life, rather than death. Let's think of love rather than loss."

"Play me a song," he said. "Play *My Happy Uncertainty*. You know, the one you were playing when I knocked myself out at the club."

She got up from his side and walked over to the piano. A short while later her music filled the air. Tom smiled as she sang the song in Portuguese about a blissful, if uncertain future with her fictional lover.

Halfway through the song, Tom got to his feel and walked over to her side as she played. At first, he stood behind her with his hands lightly resting on his shoulders, but then he pulled her to her feet and kissed her tenderly on the lips. Once more his soul thrilled to the feel of her in his arms and he vowed that come what may, he would spend the entirety of the rest of his life, however short that entirety may be, making Adriana Fernandez a happy woman.

"You know," he told her with a grin, as they quietly separated from one another, "those guys who want to buy the Jazzy Truth and turn it into a shopping center can go to hell. You know what we're gonna do, Addy?"

She found his excitement contagious. "What are we gonna do, Tom?"

"You and I, Addy, we're going to keep the club running!"

She squealed with delight. He picked her up in his strong arms, swung her feet up off the floor and twirled a waltz with her around the living room, his lips locked to hers all the while.

CHAPTER 46

Three months down the line, Tom's eyes gave out almost completely.

By then, he was legally blind, able to perceive only the barest minimum of motion. His visual world had become one huge gray blur, so much so that it no longer mattered if he opened or shut his eyes. His headaches also became more frequent, but just as before, a higher dose of medication coped with them.

Then, one Sunday night, Tom had his first seizure. The seizure began as a gentle pressure at the back of his head, which then spread like fingers around his skull and squeezed. He experienced a moment of suppressed pain, and then blacked out. When he awoke again, he was sweating. He had the knowledge that a lot of time had passed in the interim, but as it was the middle of the night and he didn't want to wake up Adriana, who was soundly asleep beside him, he couldn't tell how long he'd been out for.

Just as he had earlier done with Maggie, Tom kept the knowledge to himself. It was a given that he would soon die; there was no point in worrying Adriana with a series of false alarms.

***

They had reopened the Jazzy Truth the weekend after Joao's death. Adriana had refused to enter her former apartment since that fateful day. She'd had the same reaction to seeing Joao's blood on the floor as she had to seeing Mario's—a torrent of bad feelings associated with that spot.

Such was the strangeness of Adriana and Joao's story, that the Lifetime Channel had already commissioned a made-for-TV movie about it, called 'From Brazil with Hate.'

The Jazzy Truth was doing better than good. Possibly because of the killings that had happened there, possibly simply because once Tom put Adriana in charge of the place, she went all out to make a success of it, within a month of its reopening, people were queuing up outside the building on concert nights.

Tom had already applied to the city planners for permission to build an extension to the building to accommodate more people.

One of the most memorable performance nights occurred when Jerry Bennet, the previous resident jazzer at the club, brought his band over as part of their tour of West Virginia. That night—thankfully recorded for posterity in HD video—Adriana jammed with Jerry and his band, leading to an endless sequence of debates as to which of them was the better piano player. The YouTube upload of the concert also led to serious recording company interest in Adriana.

***

And Tom? Tom simply sat and enjoyed the music. He couldn't see anymore, but he let his ears be his new windows to the world.

He loved Adriana and she loved him. Together they made a wonderful personal music which most who knew them envied.

As a special surprise to Adriana on her 30th birthday, Tom flew in her mother from Brazil for a visit. The sounds of joy that accompanied the pair's surprise reunion delighted him and gave him almost incalculable delight.

And so, their happy days went on. Yes, the Grim Reaper was waiting with his scythe and his stopwatch, but in the meantime Tom and Adriana lived and loved with all the gusto they could find in themselves.

Sometimes, Tom felt he'd been unfaithful to Maggie and unfair to her memory, by taking up with another woman so soon after her death.

But then he comforted himself with the thought that Maggie would have approved of the replacement for her that he'd chosen.

"Don't worry, Maggie honey, I'll be with you again soon enough," he always told himself then with a broad grin.

CHAPTER 47

Tom also successfully concealed his second seizure from Adriana, and the third one too, but the fourth one happened right in front of her, just after she'd parked their car in front of the house.

When Tom revived again, he could hear the anguish in Adriana's voice. He was horizontal and realized he was in a hospital bed.

"How long was I out for?" he asked in a calm voice, not wanting to alarm her even more.

"Three hours. I thought you weren't coming back to me." She leaned on him, and her tears wet his face. "I knew you were being treated here in this specialist clinic, so once you blacked out, I immediately backed the car out of the driveway and brought you here myself."

Tom nodded and smiled. "Please call Dr. Hollis for me," he requested.

"You were lucky this time," Dr. Hollis said when he arrived at Tom's bedside. "I'm very surprised that we were able to revive you. But, Tom, your tumor is now at a very advanced stage, and to be perfectly frank with you, you could go at any minute."

Tom received this grim news calmly, the man he was conversing with nothing more than a dark blur on a gray surface. "Doc, does it make any difference if I remain in hospital? Can you keep me alive?"

"To be perfectly honest, no, we can't. All we can do is relieve your pain. Are you in any pain, Tom?"

He shook his head. "No pain, doc, the drugs work fine. But I'd like to go home, if I may. I'd rather die at home with Adriana by my side than in a hospital bed."

"That's fine," Dr. Hollis agreed.

CHAPTER 48

As Adriana shepherded him out through the clinic doors, Tom paused for a minute.

"You know, I'm sorry to put you through all of this," he apologized to Adriana. "I can't help but feel I've been incredibly selfish to drag you into my messed-up situation."

She hugged him warmly. "You've nothing to be sorry for, darling. Every second of our time together has been worth it." They resumed walking and she led him to their car. He stumbled as she was helping him into the car, and then stood beside the vehicle, leaning on the opened door.

"I feel like I'm not really here on Earth anymore," he told Adriana. "I want to remain here with you, loving you forever, but the pressure is building up in my head, almost like it's trying to force me out of my body."

She gave him a worried look. "You think you're about to have another seizure?"

He nodded. "I feel the same way I did before the last one hit me."

Adriana turned. "Wait here, I'll fetch some nurses with a stretcher."

Tom restrained her with a hand on her arm. "No. If it's time for me to leave; I'll leave quietly, without making a fuss about it. Besides, you just heard what the doc said—there's nothing they can do for me. Nothing at all. I'm terminal." He smiled. "When I die, Addy, I want to be with you when I go. I don't want it to be that you stepped outside for a cup of coffee and I've left before you get back."

Adriana sighed loudly. Ever since that fateful day when they'd professed their love for one another, she'd dreaded this moment. She wanted to break down in tears and scream, but instead she remained calm. It was Tom's calm that calmed her. If he, who was fated to die shortly could be this brave, why couldn't she be too?

I'll be brave for him. I'll be brave for both of us.

She helped him into the car, helped him fasten his seatbelt, and then walked around to the driver's side and climbed in also.

Her look at his face after starting the car alarmed her. He looked like he would depart from her any minute.

"Listen, Tom," she told him as she set the car in motion.

"I'm listening, honey."

"What would you like to do if you could only do one more thing?" Adriana asked him as they left the clinic parking lot. "Just tell me, darling. You know I'm willing to do anything I can to help you."

"Take me back to the club. I just want to hear you play one last time."

He was smiling as he said this and a responding smile crossed her face, though her smile was sad where his was peaceful.

"Of course, darling, let's go to our club," she replied. "I'd love to play for you forever and a day."

"I'd really love that," Tom said. "I really would. For me that would be the greatest gift in the whole wide world."

With tears spilling down her face, Adriana drove them both over to the Jazzy Truth.

CHAPTER 49

Tom sat quietly, listening to Adriana play. Eddie had pulled the couch right up close to the stage for him, and Tom let his ears determine his truths.

The music Adriana played was light in Tom's darkness. He felt it leading him onward, showing him the way to go. He didn't know the way; but the music assured him all was well.

An instinct had confirmed to Tom that he had very little time left in this world, maybe less than thirty minutes, even. But this was how he wanted his life to end, with the woman he loved filling his ears and mind with her beautiful music.

Adriana finished playing a song and came to him and kissed him.

"Play more," he told her. "Play the sweetest song in the world."

Laughing sadly, she departed from him again and returned to the piano. The music resumed and Tom felt weakness coming over him, the pressure in his brain beginning to build up to something critical.

Another sweet kiss tickled his lips. "Oh, darling, play some more," he pleaded again with the kisser.

She giggled and departed, and after a few seconds, more sweet music filled the air around him.

As Adriana played those wonderful chord sequences and melodies that were fast transforming her into a jazz celebrity, the doorways to the past swung open before Tom. He stepped through those gates and . . .

Suddenly, he was young again and in a newly-opened club, not his own club, but another club, in a time when his life was simpler and happier, and the future and its cares were just hazy dreams. He was one of many dancing, dancing the night away.

There in the past, he saw Adriana coming off from a performance to hug him. She let him go and as she did so, a now young-again Maggie emerged from the crowd and took his hand.

"Come with me," Maggie said in a coy voice. "The melodies are endless here!"

And on her gentle urging, the pressure filling Tom's head spilled over into eternity.

And then there was silence.

EPILOGUE

Seated there on that old couch by the stage, with love for both Adriana and Maggie in his heart, Tom Duchensky died a peaceful and happy man.

As the last seizure he would ever have sent him away into the eternal darkness from which no one returns, he smiled.

With Eddie's help, Tom had made out his will two months ago so that Adriana would have no idea of what he was doing and so not be able to dissuade him from it.

He'd left his house to his sister Sharon but had willed the Jazzy Truth club and its premises to Adriana Fernandez, along with sufficient money to make whatever improvements to the venue she felt were necessary.

He knew that in Adriana's capable hands, the Jazzy Truth's reputation and traditions would continue, that it would be a suitable memorial to Maggie.

He hoped that Adriana would find the life she deserved and thanked God he was able to have been part of hers, even though the season was short and the tragedies many.

Tom and Maggie's names might be forgotten in this world, but their spirits would live on forever in the minds of jazz lovers and, yes, Adriana was indeed capable of steering the club forward to a bright, new future. She was after all…simply amazing and Tom couldn't think of a better person for the job.

That thought was enough to put a smile on Tom's face while he died.

The End.

ABOUT THE AUTHOR

Gary Lee Vincent was born in Clarksburg, West Virginia and is an accomplished author, musician, actor, producer, director and entrepreneur. In 2010, his horror novel *Darkened Hills* was selected as 2010 Book of the Year winner by *Foreword Reviews Magazine* and became the pilot novel for *DARKENED - THE WEST VIRGINIA VAMPIRE SERIES*, that encompasses the novels *Darkened Hills, Darkened Hollows, Darkened Waters, Darkened Souls, Darkened Minds* and *Darkened Destinies*. He has also authored the bizarro thriller *Passageway*, a tribute to H.P. Lovecraft, and *When the Bedposts Shake*, an erotic horror.

Gary co-authored the novel *Belly Timber* with John Russo, Solon Tsangaras, Dustin Kay and Ken Wallace, and co-authored the novel *Attack of the Melonheads* with Bob Gray and Solon Tsangaras.

As an actor, Gary has appeared in over seventy feature films and multiple television series, including *House of Cards, Mindhunter, The Walking Dead*, and *Stranger Things*.

As a director, Gary got his directorial debut with *A Promise to Astrid*. He has also directed the films *Desk Clerk, Dispatched*, the 2020 remake of John Russo's iconic horror film *Midnight, Godsend*, and *Strange Friends*.

WHEN THE BEDPOSTS SHAKE

An Erotic Terror

GARY LEE VINCENT

WHEN THE BEDPOSTS SHAKE
(RING OF THE SUCCUBUS)

Jack Crannson was having a midlife crisis. A successful architect, Jack was more interest in running his business than saving his marriage. With his workaholic wife fueling his own disinterest, he decides to move closer to his work by purchasing an older house in the Maple Lake section of Bridgeport, West Virginia.

The house purchase seemed like a logical enough choice for Jack, despite Samantha, his estranged wife's, protest. The only illogical thing was the condition that came with the house from Mr. Bannering, the home's previous owner. . .

Mr. Bannering warned that Jack mustn't use the north bedroom, and under no circumstances, sleep in the bed. It was locked and needed to stay that way.

What Mr. Bannering failed to disclose was that trapped within that room was a demonic force, a she-devil succubus named Cali that was looking for some way to escape her prison and enter the earthly realm in the flesh to prey on male victims by feeding on their sexual energy. With the house having a new owner, she may just get her wish.

Warning: this novel contains language intended for an adult audience.

2010 Book of the Year WINNER
ForeWord Reviews Magazine

DARKENED HILLS

GARY LEE VINCENT

DARKENED HILLS
DARKENED – THE WEST VIRGINIA VAMPIRE SERIES
Book I by Gary Lee Vincent

"2010 Book of the Year WINNER"
- Foreword Reviews Magazine

A tale of gripping psychological horror!

When evil descends on a small West Virginia town, who will survive?

Jonathan did not start out his life to become a rambler, it just worked out that way. William was a troubled youth with something to hide. Both were from Melas, a small town tucked away in the West Virginia hills... a town where disappearances are happening more and more frequently.

After the suicide of a wanted serial killer, the townsfolk thought the nightmare was over. But when a centuries-old vampire is discovered they find out the hard way it's just getting started.

Dark secrets can only stay hidden for so long and when the devil comes to collect, there will be hell to pay. Can Jonathan and William find a way to stop the vampire before it's too late? Find out in Darkened Hills!

Darkened Hills is a gothic vampire novel written in the spirit of Dracula with much more sinister characters and eroticism then the old Victorian classic.

For series information, visit **www.DarkenedHills.com**.